"Down, get down!" he shouted, his voice lost amid the sound of rapid-fire gunshots and breaking glass.

Tracie could feel the impact of the bullets as they hit him, knocking the air from his body. Yet in six strides, he had her across the yard and over the old stone wall. Heath shoved her against the far side of the wall, shielding her with his body. "Stay down," he hissed, and she could hear him struggling to inhale.

She knew he was wounded—he had to be—but she couldn't see where, and the cold damp of the snow beneath her began to seep through her clothing while she waited.

Silence. Even Heath's labored breathing had eased, though his body was tense above her and he had his sidearm out, covering them, waiting. Tracie listened, not daring to move, wondering if the gunman would come after them, wondering who it could be. Her former partner's killers? Or perhaps someone who didn't want them to know the full extent of what Trevor had been involved in.

Books by Rachelle McCalla

Love Inspired Suspense

Survival Instinct
Troubled Waters

RACHELLE MCCALLA

is a mild-mannered housewife, and the toughest she ever has to get is when she's trying to keep her four kids quiet in church. Though she often gets in over her head, as her characters do, and has to find a way out, her adventures have more to do with sorting out the carpool and providing food for the potluck. She's never been arrested, or in a fistfight, or shot at. And she'd like to keep it that way! For recipes, fun background notes on the places and characters in this book and more information on forthcoming titles, visit www.rachellemccalla.com.

TROUBLED WATERS

RACHELLE McCALLA

Steeple Hill®

Published by Steeple Hill Books™

STEEPLE HILL BOOKS

Steeple
Hill®

Recycling programs
for this product may
not exist in your area.

ISBN-13: 978-0-373-67419-0

TROUBLED WATERS

www.SteepleHill.com

Printed in U.S.A.

And we know that in all things God works for the good of those who love him, who have been called according to his purpose.

—*Romans 8:28*

To my parents, Brian and Kerry Richter, with love.

ONE

Something wasn't right. Tracie Crandall eyed her new Coast Guard partner warily as they walked up the snowy path to her former partner Trevor Price's house. She felt nervous, not just because of the flint-hard, steel-blue eyes of the man walking beside her, but because it was the first time she'd been near Trevor's place since his death. Though she wasn't sure how she'd react, the last thing she wanted was to show any sign of weakness with Heath Gerlach watching.

"You've got the warrant?" Heath asked in a low voice.

Tracie patted the breast pocket of her Coast Guard parka. "Right here."

He nodded, his eyes flickering from her pocket to her face, and then quickly to the house and the woods surrounding it. Tracie felt as though he'd taken in every possible detail in those fleeting glances, and perhaps seen right through her tough exterior to her nervousness as well.

Heath's features softened ever so slightly. "You're all right coming here?"

"Of course," Tracie swallowed back her fear. "Why wouldn't I be?"

He tipped his head dismissively, his attention already back on the house. As he turned toward the curtained living room window, his nostrils flared, reminding Tracie of the way Gunnar, her German shepherd mix, reacted when he scented danger.

With her hand raised toward the doorbell, she paused, her eyes narrowing. "Do you think—" she started to ask, but the words were ripped from her lips as Heath grabbed her, scooping her off the stoop as he leapt toward the woods.

"Down, get down!" he shouted, his voice lost amid the sound of rapid-fire gunshots and breaking glass. She could feel the impact of the bullets as they hit him, knocking the air from his body. In six strides he had her across the yard and over the old stone wall that marked the property line between Trevor's lot and the woods beyond it.

Heath shoved her against the far side of the wall, shielding her with his body. "Stay down," he hissed, and she could hear him struggling to inhale. "Are you hit?"

Tracie ripped the radio from her belt. "I'm fine," she said, before hurtling a call for backup and paramedics. After hastily relaying their location and the situation, she clicked off the radio and looked back at her partner. She knew he was wounded—he had to be—but she couldn't see where, and the cold damp of the snow beneath her began to seep through her clothing while she waited.

Silence. Even Heath's labored breathing had eased, though his body was tense above her and he had his sidearm out, covering them, waiting. Tracie listened, not daring to move, wondering if the gunman would come after them, wondering who it could be. Trevor's killers? Or perhaps someone who didn't want them to know the full extent of what Trevor had been involved in.

With over six feet of solid muscle blocking her body and blocking her view, Tracie couldn't see much, but as she eased her head to the side, she saw the growing puddle of red in the snow.

"You're hit," she whispered, her voice barely louder than a breath.

"Shh," Heath cautioned her. Even in near silence, she could hear the pain in his voice.

She pinched her eyes shut, praying. The paramedics would come from the Bayfield volunteer fire association, which meant guys with beepers ditching whatever they were doing, calling in, and driving to the fire house for equipment before driving out to them. All those things took time. The roads were more or less passable after the latest snowfall, but still, she wondered if they'd be too late. She couldn't stand the idea that she'd lose two partners in less than six weeks.

"Do you need a tourniquet?" Her voice was barely audible.

Heath's head twitched slightly to one side. A quarter shake. Did he mean *no*, or was he fading already from the loss of blood? From the pattern of gunfire she'd heard, Tracie figured the gunman had been using some sort of assault rifle. Their standard-issue Coast Guard body armor wouldn't stop a bullet like that. It would barely even slow it down. And Heath had to have been hit several times.

An engine revved behind the house, and Heath eased up from above her. "He's getting away," he muttered, though his movements were still cautious, his voice quiet.

"Do you want me to try to go after him?" Tracie offered as the sound of the vehicle began to fade.

"No," Heath shifted his body and looked down at her. His face was so close she could see the tips of dark hairs starting to sprout into a five-o'clock shadow. "Your body armor won't stop what he's shooting."

About to ask how he knew, Tracie realized Heath's arm was wrapped around her torso, his hand beneath her, cradling her from the cold of the snow. "And what are you wearing?" she asked, shifting her body away from the close contact, more aware of him than she wanted to be. "Obviously not our standard-issue bulletproof vest."

"No, obviously not," Heath conceded, "or I'd be dead right now, and so would you." He turned at the distant sound of sirens.

Tracie took advantage of his distraction to assess what she could of his wounds. The red puddle seemed to be coming from his sleeve—he'd apparently been hit on his upper arm. The back of his Coast Guard parka was riddled with holes rimmed by tufts of synthetic down that was blackened by the searing force of the bullets. She swallowed hard, wondering how many had made it through. The severity of his wounds would depend on the angle and point of entry, and most importantly, what kind of vest he was wearing.

She sat up higher and reached for his arm. If he'd been hit in a major vein, he could still bleed to death before the paramedics could save him. She said a silent prayer that they'd hurry.

Heath leaned back against her, pushing her down. "Don't move until backup arrives."

"But the gunman already left," she protested.

"You don't know that."

Heath sat in the open back bay of the ambulance and tried not to wince as a medic wrapped the wound on his arm.

"I really think you should get an X-ray. You could easily have broken a rib." Another paramedic held up the severely dented steel plate they'd pulled from the back of his body armor. Six mushroomed bullets had been hiding inside—one for each of the blunt force trauma wounds he'd sustained on his back.

"And if I did, what are you going to do about it? Put me in a body cast?" Heath's eyes narrowed as he watched Tracie talking to the local sheriff across the yard. She'd stayed at his side long enough for the medics to survey his injuries and determine none of them were life-threatening. Now Heath wished he could hear what she was saying. His boss at the FBI was already bugging him for answers, but in the three days he'd been undercover as a Coast Guardsman, Heath had yet to get Tracie to talk much about Trevor Price's death. "How much longer is this going to take?"

"I'm done," the first medic said. "But I'm not letting you go until you sign these release forms. It's not my fault you won't go to the hospital."

Heath quickly scrawled his name wherever the man pointed, then slipped back into his bullet-hole-riddled parka before heading back across the crime scene.

Sheriff's deputies and his fellow Coast Guardsmen were crawling all over the house looking for clues. If there was anything to find, they'd find it. Still, he wanted to take a look around for himself. Though Trevor's house was several miles back in the woods and therefore not traditional Coast Guard territory, the Lake Superior officer's death, as well as the shady practices that had led to his death, made his house part of the Coast Guard's ongoing investigation.

Heath caught Tracie's eye and nodded to her, and she broke off her conversation with the sheriff and hurried over.

"They're letting you walk around?" She pinched her mouth into a slight smile, but her eyes still looked worried.

"Don't worry about me. I'm invincible," he assured her, with a grin to tell her he knew he wasn't quite.

Tracie's smile inched a little closer to her eyes. Heath wondered what she'd look like if she really smiled. Beautiful? No, she was that already. She'd be simply stunning. For a moment, he found himself wanting to make her smile, to laugh even, but he quickly chided himself. He was here to investigate her in conjunction with her previous partner's murder. That didn't require making her smile.

He adopted a more serious expression. "What have they found?"

"Footprints. Size fourteen, or pretty close to it.

Not too common, but not nearly rare enough. And snowmobile tracks."

"That was the engine we heard?"

She nodded. "We followed them as far as Petersons', but there are hundreds of tracks over there. He could have gone any direction—there's no way to tell."

"Right." From what Heath understood, snowmobiles were as common as cars in the Northwoods of Wisconsin, and far easier to navigate during the long winter months when traveling by road was often risky. Their gunman could be anywhere. "No other leads?"

"No sign of forced entry to the house, which seems a little strange. John and Mack had locked it up tight after their last investigation—Jim had issued them new locks. Ben and Clint are dusting for fingerprints, but in this weather, everyone wears gloves." She looked down at Heath's bare hands.

He flexed his fingers against the cold. If she was trying to nag him, she'd find she wouldn't get far. "So what's our next move?"

"It's a pretty dead end." She shrugged. "I'll see Trevor's brother, Tim, at church tomorrow and ask him if he knows of anyone who'd be at his brother's place."

"What time's the service?"

Tracie raised an eyebrow at him.

"I'll meet you there," Heath explained.

"You're on medical leave. You have a hole in your arm and blunt force trauma wounds all across your back. You're not getting out of bed tomorrow."

"Medical leave is voluntary."

Tracie huffed impatiently. "Fine, you do whatever you want, but I'm not going to be part of it." She turned and crunched away across the snow.

Heath watched her go. Interesting woman. She had a chip on her shoulder bigger than the bullet hole in his arm, which made it very difficult to get any information out of her. She was tight-lipped about her work and absolutely silent about her personal life. The tip about church was the closest he'd come to a break in the three days he'd been on the case. Which was why, even though he hadn't been to a worship service in fifteen years, he was going to go to church the next morning.

Tracie spotted Tim Price the moment she entered the small country church, and slid into the pew next to him. He smiled a greeting and then looked back down to the Bible on his lap. She felt a grateful prayer of thanks rising in her heart at the sight of Tim reading his Bible—at the sight of Tim in church at all.

The younger man had been in a rough spot when she'd first met him. Between the drugs and alcohol, it was amazing he hadn't died of an overdose long before. But when his brother, Trevor, had been shot six weeks earlier, Tim had immediately entered a treatment program and given his life back to God. She'd accompanied him to church in the city while he was in treatment, and was thrilled that he'd insisted on meeting her at church now that he was home.

Lifting her eyes to the dark wood-beamed ceiling, Tracie took a long breath and tried to clear her mind as she prepared to worship. Life had been crazy lately, and the attempt on her life the day before, though unexpected, seemed to fit all too well with her recent experiences. But here in the house of God she could be at peace, if only for an hour.

As she began to bow her head, Tracie glanced around the sanctuary at the familiar faces who shared this sacred hour with her nearly every Sunday. She stopped short when a man's broad-shouldered frame entered the room, blocking the bright sunlight that streamed through the antique leaded-glass windows.

Heath.

He'd found her. Tracie's heart stopped, then started thumping in an irregular, nervous beat. Sure, the worship service time was no great secret—he'd probably called the church and listened to the message on the answering machine.

But most people in the coastal village of Bayfield worshipped in the larger church in town. The little countryside chapel where Tracie attended services had been founded centuries before by Swedish settlers, and remained a small, tight-knit congregation largely unaffected by the tourists and transplants who'd changed the face of the larger village church. She'd have expected him to look for her in the town church, not here.

So Heath had scented her out. She tried to tell herself it was no big deal. Anybody could come to church. She knew she should be glad her new partner was a churchgoing man. Trevor had never darkened the doors of the worship space in the time she'd known him, though it would have done him a world of good, she was sure. He might even be alive today if he hadn't gotten himself involved with diamond smugglers. Rather than allow thoughts of either man to disturb her, Tracie closed her eyes and tried to breathe in the peace she'd felt before she'd spotted Heath.

But peace eluded her. She watched warily as Heath made his way across the back of the sanctuary toward where she and Tim sat. Her back stiffened, and she instinctively turned as though to shield Tim as much as possible from Heath.

What was it about her new partner that upset her so much? Was it because he'd transferred in from elsewhere? When Trevor had been murdered, she'd figured she'd fall in with someone from among the existing crew. But Jake Struckman, the Officer in Charge at the Bayfield station, had shocked her when he'd announced they were bringing in someone new to work with her.

While that news had come as a surprise, Tracie knew it didn't explain all of the unease she felt around him. She could have chalked it up to the fear she'd always felt around Trevor. Her former partner had bent a lot of rules, even broken some when he knew there was nothing she could do to stop him, and she'd learned to constantly be on her guard around him. It was possible she'd transferred her unease onto Heath.

It would have been an easy explanation, but Tracie knew that wasn't it, either. If anything, she'd been relieved to have someone new to work with. Nobody could be as awful as Trevor. And so far, in the three days she'd worked with him, Heath had been a perfect gentleman. He'd even saved her life. So it didn't stand to reason that she feared him simply because she'd feared Trevor.

No, there was something about him that made her pulse race every time she saw him. He was too quiet about himself, and too quick to ask her personal questions. He watched her too carefully. And though he'd definitely tried to downplay the difference, he was overqualified for the job, and overdressed. Nobody else in the Coast Guard wore steel-plated body armor.

To her relief, the worship service began just as Heath sat down, and Tracie was able to push her nervous thoughts away and focus on the minister's words. Whatever the issue was with Heath, the next fifty minutes wouldn't change anything. But it would change her heart, and she needed God's peace more than ever now.

Heath watched Tracie out of the corner of his eye. Though she'd obviously seen him, she'd failed to be nearly as welcoming as the parishioners who'd greeted him when he came in. In fact, her body language said she didn't want to have anything to do with him.

Fine. Heath was a patient man. He'd been waiting for her to come around since he'd arrived for his undercover position in the Coast Guard. He wished he could tell her his true identity. Normally, he'd want those working closest to him to be aware of who he was and what he was up to. But not Tracie. She was the last person who'd be allowed to know. He was there to investigate her and her colleagues for their roles in Trevor Price's murder, and to find out if anyone on the team had been involved with the diamond-smuggling ring.

The only person at the Coast Guard station who was aware of his status as an FBI agent was Jake

Struckman, the Bayfield Officer in Charge, who'd helped establish his cover. All the Coast Guardsmen seemed to accept the explanation that he was a transfer from another station, brought in because of the recent trouble they'd been having, and his expertise gained during his previous experience as a Navy SEAL. So far, no one had caught on to his total inexperience with the Coast Guard. He'd memorized the handbook and leaned on his sharp instincts to fill in the cracks. It helped that the Bayfield team were a big-hearted bunch. They'd seemed more concerned about not disappointing him than checking for any holes in his story.

Except for Tracie. She still looked at him warily and had that chip on her shoulder he couldn't yet account for. Did that mean Tracie was connected to Trevor's diamond-smuggling friends, or involved in some way in Trevor's death? If he'd read about her attitude in a report, he might have reached that conclusion. But having met her, he wasn't so sure.

No, her eyes had gone a little too wide at the sight of blood, for one thing. She'd jumped a little too high when the bullets started flying. And she'd only been wearing a lightweight bulletproof vest when the tip of the rifle had peeked through the window curtains at Trevor's. If she'd had inside knowledge, she'd have gone in prepared. But as it was, if he'd grabbed her a split-second later, Tracie would have been dead.

Heath replayed the scene through his mind in slow motion. He'd sensed something was wrong, but the gun had still taken him by surprise. His reaction had been pure training and instinct, no time to stop and think things through. Tracie had felt so light in his arms, and so delicate. He'd been surprised by the overwhelming need he'd felt to protect her.

He glanced over at her now, sitting quietly with her head bowed as the minister prayed, her bulky fisherman-style sweater doing little to disguise her slender frame. Underneath her tough exterior, he sensed that she was fragile—frightened, even. But she'd put up a thick wall to keep him out.

In order to find out what she knew, he'd have to break through that wall somehow. In the four days he'd known her, he'd figured out it wouldn't fall easily. But if he could get inside to the timid woman underneath, he might be able to convince her to lean on him.

And then? Well, then he'd have his answers, which was the whole point of this assignment. His mission would be accomplished. So why did the idea of getting close to Tracie Crandall frighten him so much?

Tracie followed Tim to the fellowship hall after the final song. She wasn't sure how to tell him what had happened at his brother's house the day before. Fortunately, she didn't have to. Tim had already heard.

"I'm so glad you weren't injured. The first I heard, nobody knew which Coasties had been involved in the shooting, but I had a sense you were one of them. I even called your house, but you weren't home yet."

"You could have left a message." Tracie wouldn't have minded the excuse to call and talk to him sooner.

"I didn't want to bother you." Tim clutched a cup of coffee without drinking from it.

"Don't worry about bothering me," she patted his free arm. "You're my friend."

"Right." His eyes darted about the room. Though he'd been off drugs for weeks, he still had a jumpy, disjointed manner about him. He leaned a little closer and lowered the volume of his voice. "I've been asking some questions."

"Questions?"

"Some of Trevor's old buddies. Somebody has to have heard something."

Though part of her didn't want Tim doing any investigative work on his own, Tracie felt partly relieved he'd taken the initiative. Tim had contacts she had no other way of reaching, but she'd never feel comfortable asking him to get in touch with them for her. "And?" she prompted.

"Hello, Tracie." Heath had snuck up on her.

Tim pinched his mouth shut.

Tracie could have kicked her new partner. "Hello, Heath." She knew she needed to introduce Heath to Tim, but she didn't know how to break it to Tim that Heath had replaced his older brother. "Tim, have you met—?"

"No," Tim shifted his coffee to his other hand. "You're Heath, right?"

"Heath Gerlach," her new partner shook Tim's hand. "And you're Tim Price."

"Yes. Trevor's little brother."

"I'm sorry to hear about your loss."

"Thank you."

The men maintained eye contact, and Tracie tried hard to read what passed between them. Animosity? No, Tim was too pure of heart since his conversion to sink to that. She didn't even sense a competitive spirit. In fact, they almost seemed to share understanding. Sympathy. Tracie felt herself softening ever so slightly toward Heath. She didn't nearly trust him, but he'd demonstrated a rare sensitivity toward her grieving friend. It was far more than she'd expected.

Now she just had to figure out how to get rid of Heath so Tim would finish telling her what he'd learned.

"You're filling my brother's slot on the force,

hmm?" Tim raised his cup to his lips, his face curious, his tone without guile.

"He's left me some pretty big shoes to fill," Heath offered.

"Size fourteen, to be exact," Tim offered.

Tracie chuckled along with them, her mind immediately latching on to Trevor's shoe size. The same as the footprints they'd found at his house. But he'd been dead for over a month. Could the footprints have been that old? Impossible— far too much snow had fallen since then. Could their gunman have slipped on a pair of Trevor's boots to throw them off his trail? It was certainly a possibility.

She was so intrigued by the idea, she didn't pay attention to what the men were discussing until she heard Tim saying, "As I was just telling Tracie, I've been in contact with some of Trevor's friends."

"But I thought everyone involved in the diamond smuggling had been caught," Heath said, his words taking Tracie back to the final showdown on Devil's Island six weeks before—right after Trevor's death.

"Everyone involved," Tim repeated, his eyes darting around the room. He lowered his voice and leaned in closer to the two of them. "You must not realize how deep this thing goes."

"Why don't you enlighten me?" Heath's quiet voice remained casual.

Tim shrugged. "I'm meeting with some guys tonight. I don't know if I'll learn anything, but if you guys to stop by my place tomorrow, say around noon, I'll tell you everything I know."

"Tomorrow at noon then." Heath graciously raised his coffee cup to Tim, then took a sip and walked away.

Tracie watched him go, her insides roiling with a mixture of frustration and distrust.

Tim's words pulled her from her thoughts. "He seems nice."

"Yes." Tracie admitted. "He does." Almost too nice.

Heath called Jonas Goodman as soon as he got back to his apartment.

"Tim Price is talking."

"Really?" his FBI supervisor actually sounded impressed for once. "And what's he saying?"

"I don't know yet. We're meeting him tomorrow at noon. I'll call you afterward."

"Are you sure you're up to this? I received your medical report last night. Those bruises on your back look ugly."

"They're even uglier today, but that's not going to stop me. This case is cracking, and that gunman yesterday has me convinced whatever's going down here is big. You don't pull out an assault rifle unless you're pretty desperate."

"Or pretty stupid." Jonas noted. "Remember, we are working with crooks here."

"Crooks who successfully imported synthetic diamonds and passed them off as the real thing for over a decade," Heath reminded his boss. "Hardly the work of a jumpy amateur."

Jonas let the remark slide. "What about the girl? Got any dirt on her?"

"Tracie?" Heath bristled at his boss's choice of words. "She's clean so far."

"Then dig deeper. She was way too tight with Trevor not to be involved with his business. We need to catch the remaining smugglers who are still out there. She has to know something."

Heath's hand tightened on his phone. "How do you know that? Do you have information you haven't passed on to me?"

"Of course not. But everything points to her."

Heath wanted to defend Tracie, but he checked his emotions. Why did he feel so strongly about her? He couldn't give a solid reason. "Okay," he relented. "I'm on it."

"Good. If you're going to crack this case, you'll need to crack her first. But I don't think that will be too difficult for you."

Heath hesitated. "Could you clarify that statement?"

The insinuation in Jonas's voice carried clearly over the phone. "She's a young woman working a lonely job. You're an attractive man." He cleared his throat. "Don't worry about fallout. You do what you have to do. We'll clean up afterward."

Heath's throat tightened as he realized what his boss was openly hinting at. He'd always enjoyed working under Jonas Goodman, who had a reputation as a maverick, and whose unorthodox tactics never failed to make his job more interesting. But a sick pit churned in his stomach as he realized how much more complicated his job description now was. He'd killed before. In his line of work, it was a given. But he'd never broken a woman's heart.

"Heath?" Jonas spoke into the silence. "Do we have an understanding?"

"Yes, sir."

"Good. I expect a full report tomorrow. And I don't like disappointment."

"Yes, sir." Heath's throat felt dry. He ended the call and pinched his eyes shut, one single image filling his mind.

Tracie. He'd saved her life the day before, and still felt a lingering need to protect her from harm, to find out what had caused fear to haunt her eyes and to save her from whatever troubled her. And now Jonas wanted him to intentionally hurt her.

Clenching his jaw, Heath stood and paced the room. Tracie was his target. He had to break through her defenses, find out what she knew, and report back to Jonas in less than twenty-four hours.

He'd never had an assignment like this one, and he already knew Tracie wouldn't open up to him easily. Still, he had a sense that getting close to her wouldn't be the most difficult part of his new mission.

No, the hardest part would be forgiving himself afterward.

TWO

Tracie had her head in the cupboard and was evaluating her dinner choices when the phone rang. She held a box of cereal in one hand and a can of ravioli in the other, and set down the pasta to answer.

"Hello?"

Heath's voice caught her off guard. "Have you had dinner yet?"

She looked at the box of cereal. "Not quite."

"Care to join me? I'm sorry for the late notice, I just…" he paused.

She waited.

"I've eaten every meal by myself since I've been here, and I thought it might be nice not to have to do that, for a change."

His words struck a chord, and Tracie felt an emptiness inside that was more than just her stomach growling. She couldn't remember when she'd last shared a meal with another person. But she didn't know Heath very well, and memories of her previous partner's unprofessional behavior toward her set off warning bells. "I make it a personal policy not to fraternize with my coworkers when I'm off duty." She was glad she'd established that before Trevor had gotten out of hand.

"Oh." Disappointment resonated over the phone. "You wouldn't make an exception for my sake?"

She hesitated. The man had saved her life. But her policy had saved her skin before, too. "No exceptions."

"Right. Sorry to bother you. Goodbye then."

"'Bye." Tracie hung up the phone and leaned back against the cupboard. Gunnar, her German shepherd mix, whimpered in concern at her feet, and she realized she was clutching the cereal box so tightly to her chest that she'd crumpled it.

She looked at the box, then down at her dog. "It's okay. I'm fine." She forced a smile for Gunnar's benefit, but he didn't look any more convinced than she felt. Shaking off her doubts, she nodded resolutely and proceeded to pour herself a bowl of cereal. "That was the right answer. I'm pretty sure it was."

Tracie pulled up at the Coast Guard station the next morning just as Heath was getting out of his truck. Her insides knotted at the sight of him.

"Medical leave," she said with a pointed look at the bandage on his arm.

He grinned at her, and she felt her heart give a dip. "Not for me, thanks. How was your dinner?"

It had been horribly dissatisfying, and she'd ended up feeling so bad about turning him away that she hadn't even been able to finish her cereal, which had seemed to stick halfway down her throat every time she tried to swallow. But she wasn't about to tell him that. "It's really none of your business," she reminded him as she stepped through the door he held open for her.

"Mine too," he agreed.

"What?" She spun and looked at him, meeting his eyes, where flickering sadness didn't match the smile he'd pasted on his lips.

"Dinner," he explained, letting the fake smile drop. "Lonely and disappointing."

"I didn't say that."

"You didn't have to."

Tracie's heart thumped hard against her rib cage and she hurried to the office that housed her cubicle, hoping he'd disappear into his own. Instead, he followed her.

"Look, I don't mean to be rude," she stared him down, "but I have work to do."

"*We* have work to do."

"I don't need your help completing my paper-work."

"The paperwork can wait, Princess. Somebody tried to kill us on Saturday, and I intend to catch whoever it was before they get a chance to finish the job."

Tracie bristled. She was no princess. Princesses didn't work for the Coast Guard. "Look, Heath, I'd love to catch our gunman, but we have no idea who it is, and no leads right now to go on." She sat at her desk and picked up a sheaf of papers.

"And we're not going to find any leads sitting around doing paperwork." Heath plucked the papers from her hands and set them out of her reach on top of her file cabinets.

She narrowed her eyes at him. "Then what do you propose?"

"Have you had breakfast?"

"No," Tracie stood. "Not that it's any of your business." She gestured for him to leave. "I have work to do."

Heath smiled as he stepped out of the office. "I'll be back."

Twenty minutes later, Heath stepped, uninvited, into Tracie's cubicle and plunked a fresh apple frit-ter on her desk, then slid a steaming cup of coffee next to it. "Half cream, no sugar," he smiled tri-umphantly. "Jake ratted you out."

"I had no idea Jake cared so much," Tracie slid the coffee toward her, lifted the lid, and inhaled a deep breath of steam.

"From the Egg Toss Café," Heath explained, hoping he'd earn points for fetching her favorite brew.

"I can see that." She speared an icy eyebrow his way, but took a small swallow and reached for the fritter. "Have a seat," she said, nodding toward the spare chair as she took a big bite of the pastry. "Tell me what I have to do to make you go away."

Inwardly congratulating himself on his small victory, Heath took the chair and opened a white sack, pulling out another fritter for himself. "I want to know everything you know about Trevor."

She shrugged and washed down a bite with coffee. "It's in the report. Read it."

"I've read it. I can quote long sections from memory, if you'd like. But nothing in the report tells me who else Trevor was involved with, or why they'd rather risk a murder charge than let me look at a house your men had already searched." The vivid details of the report stood out fresh in his mind, from the moment Tracie and two civilians discovered Trevor's body floating facedown in Lake Superior, to their discovery of a hidden cave under Devil's Island. But the body had disappeared before they could recover it.

Tracie leveled her gaze at him across the desk. "Don't you think I'd tell you if I had any idea? It's not in my best interest to withhold information, you know."

"But you were closer to Trevor than anyone else on this team."

"We really weren't that close." She plucked a large blob of apple from the fritter, and dropped the gooey mess into her mouth.

As Heath watched her lips close over the morsel, he was struck again by how attractive the woman sitting across from him really was. What was she doing living in this tiny dot on the map, working for the Coast Guard of all things? It took him several seconds to pull his thoughts back to their conversation. "How long had you known Trevor before his death?"

Tracie sighed over her fritter. "I'm from Bayfield. Trevor's from Bayfield, too, but he's a few years older than I am. Growing up, I'd heard his name, but never paid too much attention to him. When I started working for the Coast Guard, he was stationed elsewhere, near Canada, I guess. He transferred here, we started working together. What else do you want to know? He took his coffee with cream and way too much sugar. He'd eat pretty much anything, including other people's food if they didn't eat it first. I think he felt entitled to things, but I never understood why." She shrugged and took another bite of apple fritter.

Heath felt like he was beginning to make progress. "And you had no idea he was involved with a diamond-smuggling ring?"

"None," Tracie looked at him blankly and swallowed. "As far as I know, *nobody* had any idea anyone was smuggling anything through the Apostle Islands. Nobody even knew there was a sea cave hideout in Devil's Island—not unless you believed the old fishermen's tales about pirates, anyway. Six weeks ago, the case got blown wide open. Before that, I admit I was completely oblivious."

"So you never suspected Trevor was involved in anything covert?"

"No." Tracie looked annoyed. "Why would I?"

"You spent ten hours a day together, four days a week. He never did anything suspicious in all that time?"

"Look, Trevor and I had an arrangement. He stayed at his desk, I stayed at mine. When we drove around in the truck together or rode around in the boat, he drove and I navigated. He did the grunt work and I did the thinking, and we never talked about our personal lives. Ever. It's an arrangement I'm hoping you and I can duplicate."

"But you're friends with his little brother." Heath persisted.

"I met Tim *after* Trevor was already dead, when Tim came forward with information that helped us crack the case. We've barely known each other a month. And yes, I'm already better friends with Tim than I ever was with Trevor, but that only reinforces how very little I cared for Trevor."

"So you didn't like him?"

Tracie threw back her head and looked at the ceiling. Heath watched the muscles in her slender neck shift as she tightened her jaw in frustration. "Trevor and I had an arrangement," she repeated.

"What kind of arrangement?"

Heath watched carefully as Tracie's eyes darted to the door, as though seeking escape. Her face paled slightly and a vessel in her neck began to pulse visibly. She stood. "I think it's time for you to leave."

Though Heath rose from his chair, he didn't take his eyes off Tracie's face. He was learning more by watching her reaction to his question than he'd gathered from anything she'd told him in the last five days. She was scared. Of Trevor? He had to know.

"What was your arrangement with Trevor?" he asked quietly.

"I just told you." The fire had gone out of her voice. Her chin quivered ever so slightly.

"So you never saw him outside of work?"

"Leave," she pointed to the door. She wasn't ordering him anymore. Her eyes were pleading.

Heath felt an unfamiliar urge to soothe her. "Tracie." He spoke her name softly.

She flinched as he drew closer.

And suddenly, Heath realized he had to back off. "I'm sorry. I'm out of here." He glanced back as he slipped through the door. Tracie's face was still turned away, and her slight shoulders heaved as she gulped a breath.

For a fleeting instant, he wanted to grab her up into his arms, to protect her from harm as he had on Saturday. But something told him he was already too late.

Trevor had gotten to her first.

It took Tracie most of the rest of the morning to compose herself. Heath showed up at her desk shortly before noon. He handed her the keys. "Why don't you drive? You know the way."

She accepted them with quiet thanks and tried not to shiver when his hand touched hers. His comment on the phone the night before had reminded her of how rarely she experienced human contact. But she didn't need to get it from him. She had friends. Tim was one of them.

Tim's place was on the edge of town, rimmed by woods like so much of northern Wisconsin. Tracie spotted his bike leaning against the side of the porch. She knew he hadn't driven since his license had been revoked following a drunk-driving charge the year before. She smiled. Tim was a good guy. A lot of drunks just kept on driving without a license.

Heath followed her up the peeling porch steps, and Tracie felt a sense of déjà vu as she recalled what had happened two days before when she and Heath had stood on a Price doorstep. She shook off her nervousness, rang the bell, and waited. No answer. She met Heath's eyes, he shrugged, and she pressed the buzzer again. Still nothing.

"The bell might be out. Let me try knocking." Heath reached past her and rapped on the doorframe.

"Here, try the inside door," Tracie suggested, alert to the possibility of danger, and eager to get inside instead of standing out in the open on the porch. She held the storm door open.

Hardly had Heath's knuckles touched the inner door than it swung inward. Heath quickly reacted and raised his arm. "Don't look—" he started.

But Tracie had already seen inside. Tim lay in a pool of blood on the floor.

"Tim!" Tracie gasped as she shouldered past Heath to her fallen friend. Her hand flew to his neck and found a weak pulse. Hope rose within her. "He's alive!" She could hear Heath behind her, giving instructions over his radio. "We need a medical team, quickly!"

"Tracie?" Tim's eyelids fluttered.

"Yes, Tim, I'm right here." She found the wound in his gut and tried to stem the flow of blood. "Help is on the way. Hang in there."

"Can you hear them?"

Tracie listened for the sound of approaching sirens, though it was far too soon to expect them to arrive. The only sounds she could hear were Heath's soft footfalls as he scoured the perimeter behind her. "Not yet, Tim, but they're on their way."

"They're singing," Tim gasped. "So beautiful." His eyes bore a faraway look.

And suddenly Tracie realized Tim was no longer really with her. "Tim," she choked on his name. "Tim, stay with me. Look at me!" she demanded.

Tim shifted his gaze to her face, and his pupils dilated as he focused on her.

"Who did this to you?" Tracie could feel the tears running down her cheeks. She realized Tim didn't have much time. Likely the only way they'd ever bring his killer to justice was if he could name him before he died.

Tracie watched the light fade from his eyes.

"No, Tim. Look at me! Who did this?"

Tim blinked. "T—" he choked. "T-Tre—"

Tracie focused, pleading with her eyes.

"—verrrr." The last syllable escaped his mouth in a sigh.

And he was gone.

Tracie picked up his hand and held it to her lips. "No." She tried to squeeze back the tears. "No, please, no."

She didn't realize Heath stood behind her until she felt his hand on her back.

"Perimeter's clear," he said softly.

Tracie nodded. She didn't look up at Heath, but neither did she push his hand away. It wasn't until the paramedics came rushing in that she stood and turned to face him.

"We shouldn't have left him alone. We should have put him in protective custody."

"He didn't want to go," Heath reminded her. "Besides, we thought we had everybody."

"It doesn't matter!" Tracie hugged herself tightly. "We should have insisted. He could have gotten mad at us, but at least he'd still be alive." She looked back over her shoulder in time to see the medics draping a sheet over Tim's body. She pinched her eyes shut.

Heath's hand fell gently on her arm. "We can't go back in time. Don't blame yourself."

Much as Tracie would have liked to push him away, she found she couldn't bring herself to shrug off the light touch of his hand. She took a moment to steady her breathing, then looked Heath directly in the eye. "We have to catch whoever did this."

The corner of Heath's strong jaw shifted in a determined expression. "I think it was the same person who shot at us on Saturday."

"That makes sense," Tracie acknowledged, "but we don't have any evidence to link anyone to either crime."

"Don't we?" Heath moved closer to Tracie as investigators scurried around behind them, and his hand slid higher on her arm. "You asked Tim who did this. I heard his answer."

"You did?" A shudder rippled through her. "But all he said was—" She stopped and pinched her eyes shut, too afraid to speak the word out loud.

Heath's mouth moved close to her ear. "Trevor," he whispered.

She pulled back and looked at him, her eyes wide. "But what does that mean? Trevor's friends? Trevor's associates, his rivals, his enemies? We don't know what Tim was going to say."

"He said *Trevor*." Heath looked at her with an intensity that made her want to shrink away.

"Trevor's dead," she insisted in a whisper. Didn't Heath understand? She'd seen Trevor's dead body floating in Lake Superior. There was no way a dead man could commit murder.

"His body was never recovered," Heath challenged her.

Tracie shook her head, still feeling shell shocked. "Trevor's dead," she repeated.

Heath nodded, took a step back, and bowed his head. When he looked back up at her, his eyes wore an unreadable look. "Right." He said simply. "Right."

Jonas sounded frustrated when Heath finally reached him by phone later that afternoon to report on what had happened.

"He was still alive when you reached the house?" his supervisor clarified.

"Barely," Heath conceded. "If we'd have gotten there a moment later, we wouldn't know anything. As it was, I think it's pretty clear he was blaming his brother for his death, but Tracie doesn't necessarily see things that way."

"Ah," Jonas's tone brightened. "The two of you are close now, hmm?"

Heath cringed. "She's not the most open and trusting person, but I think she's starting to let me in." He thought about the brief time she'd allowed him to rest his hand on her arm. It wasn't much—for most people, he wouldn't think of it as anything. But with Tracie, it was progress.

"Starting to?" Frustration edged back into Jonas's tone. "Look, we've got a gunman on the loose and we've just lost a witness. We don't have time for you to ease your way into this. Tracie

Crandall knows way more than she's telling, and until we learn what she knows, we run the risk of losing more lives on this, maybe yours." Jonas paused, and his voice dropped an octave to take on bone-chilling seriousness. "If you can't handle this, Heath, tell me now, and I'll put in someone who can."

"I'm on it."

Tracie took a long soak in the tub, but she couldn't seem to wash away the chill she felt after watching Tim pass away in her arms. She dressed in her comfiest yoga pants and an oversized sweatshirt, and joined Gunnar in the kitchen, where her bare cupboards offered little to console her. Even Gunnar whined when she poured him the same old dry dog food.

"Sorry, buddy," she whispered when he looked up at her with pleading eyes.

She jumped at the sound of the doorbell. "You expecting anyone?" she asked the dog.

Gunnar cocked his head to the side and barked once before trotting off toward the front door. Tracie followed him and flipped the switch for the porch light. The broad-shouldered silhouette at the door appeared to be holding a pizza box. Tracie let go of the breath she hadn't realized she'd been holding.

She looked down at her dog. "I didn't order pizza. You?"

Gunnar ignored her and poked his head through the doggie door.

Taking her cue from her dog, Tracie drew closer and peeked tentatively through the sheer curtains.

"It's me. Heath," her partner mouthed as he peered back at her through the gap in the shades.

Tracie jumped back and opened the door. "What are you doing here?" She grabbed Gunnar by the collar before he could attack.

Heath stepped into the house holding the pizza above his head. "Since you turned me down last night, I decided tonight I wouldn't bother to ask." He looked at her with challenge in his eyes.

Tracie hardly noticed his look. Instead she stared at her dog, who was nuzzling Heath's free hand playfully while the Coast Guardsman attempted to pet him.

"Beautiful," Heath nodded to Gunnar. "Part Great Dane?"

"Mostly German shepherd, I think."

"But bigger," Heath noted.

"Uh-huh." Tracie looked quizzically at Gunnar. "He likes you," she said softly.

"You sound surprised. Should I be insulted?"

"Oh. No." Tracie shook her head and tried to focus her thoughts. "It's just that—" She stopped. She needed to convince Heath to leave, but at the same time, the pizza smelled so delicious. Her stomach growled.

"What?"

"Gunnar hated Trevor," she admitted in a small voice.

"Gunnar—" Heath looked down at the dog with a bright smile "—you're a smart dog." He crouched a little lower, still holding the box high above his head.

Instead of leaping up and snatching away the pizza as she'd have expected, Gunnar planted his front paws on Heath's knees and licked his chin.

Swallowing her surprise, Tracie took a deep breath and prepared to tell Heath to leave. But the savory aroma of the pizza tickled her nostrils, and her stomach gave another grumble. She looked at her dog. Gunnar thought Heath was okay. And the day had certainly been an exceptionally trying one. Perhaps she could relax her rule just a little, under the circumstances. But what good was a personal policy if she didn't always stick to it?

Heath reached back through the open front door and grabbed a two-liter bottle of Mountain Dew.

Tracie realized she'd been outmaneuvered. She tried one last protest. "Neither of us will get any sleep tonight if we drink that."

Turning the bottle so she could clearly see the label, Heath corrected her. "It's caffeine-free." He gave her another one of his bothersome grins that told her he knew he'd won. "Where can I put this?"

With a sigh, Tracie led the way to her kitchen.

THREE

Heath wished he knew how to set Tracie at ease. She ushered him through the house like a museum tour guide who hadn't learned her lines yet.

"This is my living room. Sorry about the mess."

"You weren't expecting me," Heath assured her, taking in a room that wasn't so much messy as cluttered, with built-in oak cabinetry halfway installed along the outside wall, piles of books awaiting the finished shelves and a solid-looking window bench stained but not varnished between the ceiling-high bookshelves. "Besides, it looks like the mess belongs to your handyman, not to you."

Tracie looked up at him and blushed. "I'm the handyman."

Glancing back over the cabinetry, Heath took in the solid craftsmanship. "I'm impressed. It looks like you know what you're doing."

"I don't, really." Tracie tucked a few tools discretely on a shelf.

Heath noticed the brand name of the drill just before she set it aside. Gerlach Tools—his family's business. Fighting back the urge to look closer and see what line the drill came from, he continued on as Tracie led him through the room to her kitchen. No, it wouldn't do at all to give away that much of his identity. If she knew who he really was, she might ask how he got into the military, and he didn't feel at all confident that he could maintain his cover story if she began to ask him personal questions. Too much of his real-life history didn't match up with his cover story. The last thing he needed was to blow his cover.

Heath learned all manner of interesting tidbits from Tracie about life in the Coast Guard. He found out what to do when the copier jammed up, whom to call when a toilet backed up and how best to lie low when Jake got fired up. But he couldn't seem to steer their conversation toward anything personal, not without Tracie heading him off, going silent or even leaving the room to check the porch light or investigate imaginary noises in the basement.

He ran into a little more success when he brought the conversation around to the topic of the diamond smugglers. It seemed she was as intrigued as anyone about how they'd run their operation under everyone's noses for so long.

"None of the men we've captured will tell us anything—where the diamonds are coming from, or how they've been transporting them. The boats we captured contained a small number of stones— a few handfuls. Nothing like the reports we've heard from gemologists. They claim these fake rocks have taken over a major niche in the market. People have been paying top dollar for them for years, thinking they were getting real diamonds of superior color and clarity." She tossed a pizza crust to Gunnar before helping herself to another piece.

Heath smiled, glad to see her enjoying the food he'd brought. Tracie looked like she'd skipped too many meals. He tried to keep his tone casual, to keep her talking about the smugglers without getting suspicious of his curiosity and clamming up. But as he'd suspected, the woman who'd worked so hard to keep him at a distance had a flood of thoughts and theories pent up inside her. As she began to trust him, her dam began to crack.

"What I don't understand," she continued after she'd washed down a bite of pizza with a swig of soda, "is why no one figured out something was wrong a long time ago. I mean, we no sooner discover these smugglers than *multiple* gemologists come forward and announce these fakes have been out there for over a decade. Granted, the diamonds were excellent imitations—chemically and optically identical to real diamonds. But how could synthetics sneak by so long on the national market? And why can't the Feds figure out where they got them from? You don't just buy diamonds out of thin air. *Somebody* had to sell them. Can't they follow the trail?"

"I believe the FBI is on the case now," Heath said, trying to distance himself from the very organization he worked for. "I should hope we'd have answers soon."

Tracie let out a snort. "Not soon enough for Tim," she said, winging a pizza crust through the air and watching Gunnar leap artfully to catch it. Her scowl faded and she grinned at the dog, but when she glanced over at Heath, she immediately blushed. "I probably shouldn't give him people food, but when he gives me his sad-eyed begging look, I can't very well turn him away. He's my very best friend in the world. I don't know what I'd do without him." She clamped her mouth shut after that profession, which was the closest thing to personal information he'd learned all evening. She sat silently fiddling with her napkin while Heath finished the last piece of pizza.

When the two-liter was empty, the pizza box contained only crumbs and Tracie had carried their glasses to the sink, Heath realized he was going to have to pull out all the stops in order to keep from being evicted.

"Could you do me a favor?"

"What?" Tracie looked back at him from the sink, her tone unabashedly suspicious, and he could almost see the wheels turning in her head as she tried to invent a reason to make him leave.

Heath looked pointedly at his injured arm. "Could you take a look at my arm? The wound is on the back, on the underside, and I can't see it very well myself."

Concern crossed her features, but she chased the look away with one of distrust. "Why?"

"To see if it's getting infected."

"Can't you go to the doctor for that?"

"I could, if I wanted to waste half a day driving to Ashland and sitting in a waiting room." He approached her slowly until he stood beside her at the sink.

"You're supposed to be on medical leave anyway."

Heath could have reminded her that medical leave was voluntary, but instead checked their catty back-and-forth. "Tell you what—you take a look at it for me, and if it's getting infected, I'll call the doctor tomorrow."

"I guess I can't turn down an offer like that."

The way she smiled at his suggestion, Heath wondered if she'd stoop to lying to him to get him to call the doctor the next day. Hopefully it wouldn't come to that. If his ruse worked, he'd distract her from wanting to get rid of him and convince her to get close to him, instead. Jonas seemed to think it was the only way for him to learn her secrets. And Jonas was the boss.

Heath hurried to peel off the long-sleeved shirt he wore before Tracie could change her mind.

Tracie nearly gasped at the sight of Heath in a snug black T-shirt, but swallowed her exclamation while struggling to keep her expression unaffected. She'd already guessed the man worked out, but his well-developed muscles still took her by surprise, especially at close range. He was a powerfully built, handsome man. She focused her attention on the injury on his arm.

White tape secured a thick gauze bandage to his right triceps muscle on the underside of his arm toward the back, a place where it would have been nearly impossible for him to examine it himself. She tentatively reached for the dressing. "Do you want me to peel this back?"

"Yeah, go ahead and take a peek."

Stepping closer, she tugged gently on one corner of the tape. "I don't want to hurt you."

"That tape's nothing compared to what's under it."

"I suppose not," Tracie peeled back the tape and

winced at the sight of the wound underneath. "Oh."
She couldn't suppress her reaction.

"That bad?"

"It's like something took a bite out of your
arm."

"It did. Does it look infected?"

"Not really. It looks like it's healing." She peered
a little closer, close enough to smell the scent of the
antibiotic that covered the injury. Another smell
teased at her nose—something masculine and
slightly spicy. She breathed a little deeper, then
realized she was probably sniffing Heath's aftershave. Self-conscious, she took a half step back.

"I guess you don't need a doctor after all," she
noted, smoothing her hand over the tape, barely
daring to press down lest she hurt him. "There."
She slid one fingertip around the edge of the bandage to be sure it was secure. "You're all set."

"Thanks." He turned slowly to face her. He stood
too close, and his expression was intense, his eyes
smoldering.

Tracie felt overwhelmed. It had been such a long
day. Her nerves had been shot long before he'd
shown up on her porch with pizza, and her mind
was still muddled from dinner. Talking to him
had eased a weight off her shoulders. It had made
her feel closer to him, too. Now he stood mere
inches from her with a look on his face she'd never

seen before, yet somehow she knew exactly what it meant.

She took a deep breath and tried to clear her thoughts, but instead found herself breathing in more of the faded scent he wore. "You smell good." The words escaped from her mouth before she even realized she'd been consciously thinking them.

"So do you." His fingers touched her hair where it hung past her chin.

About to deny it, she realized what he was referring to. "Oh, my shampoo."

"It smells fruity. Strawberries?" He leaned closer to her, his nose nearly brushing her temple as he inhaled her scent.

"No, passion fruit," she blurted, and immediately blushed. There was no way she could let whatever was happening between them continue. He was getting too close. She took a step back. "Sorry. You just smell so much better than Trevor."

"How did Trevor smell?" Heath must have sensed her discomfort, because he grabbed his other shirt and pulled it back on.

"Awful," she said emphatically, hoping to bury whatever had just happened under a mountain of words. "He wore this ridiculous, expensive cologne. I asked him about it once because it was so strong, and he told me how much he paid for it. I don't remember what he said it cost, but it was a *lot*, and he always used way too much so that it followed him in a cloud. I've never smelled anything like it before or since. Except—" She caught herself a moment too late and stopped.

"Except what?" Heath's steel-blue eyes watched her as several seconds ticked by. "Don't tell me it was nothing. You were going to say something. You've never smelled anything like Trevor's cologne except *what?*"

"It really was nothing," Tracie sighed.

"Then it shouldn't be any big deal for you to tell me."

"It's not even worth telling."

"Prove it. Tell me and I'll tell you if it was worth telling or not."

Tracie's tired mind spun as she tried to follow Heath's logic. She felt completely exhausted: mentally, physically, and especially emotionally. "Fine. I smelled Trevor's cologne at his house on Saturday, just before we were shot at. But how can that mean anything? It was *his house*. He wore so much of that stuff it was bound to linger even though he's been dead for over a month. The smell will probably never come out of his carpets." She planted her hands on her hips and looked up at him. "So see? It really was nothing."

"And that's all?"

Tracie wanted to nod, to claim there had never been anything more to what she was thinking, but she couldn't lie to him. "And I smelled it at

Tim's house this morning. Very faintly. I was so distracted by everything else I didn't even think about it until just now, but I guess it makes sense. Tim was Trevor's brother. Why wouldn't his place carry a little bit of his smell?"

"Had you smelled it before when you'd gone over there?"

"I'd only been twice before."

"And you smelled it there then?"

Tracie hesitated.

Heath took a step closer to her, and his hand fell on her arm.

She felt the warmth of his touch run straight to her heart.

"No," she admitted reluctantly. "Today was the first time."

"Thank you for telling me." Heath leaned toward her and whispered the words, his eyes meeting hers, his hand still on her arm.

Tracie nearly looked away, but there was something in his expression that told her he wasn't out to hurt her like Trevor always had been. For a moment, she allowed herself to bask in the reassuring feeling that she wasn't alone on this case—that Heath was working on her side. Was Heath really someone she could trust? She wanted so much to believe it was true.

Gunnar's sharp barking brought her back to reality, and she looked down to see her dog nosing Heath in the leg, obviously trying to push him away.

"Looks like we've got a chaperone," Heath said softly, stepping back and pulling his hand away.

Tracie didn't know how to respond. She knew she ought to be glad her dog had the good sense to break them apart before they got any closer, but as reality returned with its crushing weight, she almost considered offering to put the dog out in the yard. But now that they were no longer standing so close, Gunnar didn't seem nearly as concerned. He hunkered down and put his head on her left foot, as though staking his claim.

Her silence must have concerned Heath, because he quickly apologized. "I'm sorry. I know you said you don't fraternize with coworkers. I should respect your personal space."

"It's okay," she said softly.

A relieved grin spread across Heath's lips. "I'm glad. I think I'd like to spend more time with you."

Though she hadn't intended to encourage him, Tracie couldn't help smiling back at him. She shook her head and whispered, mostly to herself, "I should know better."

"Why? There's no rule in the Coast Guard against the two of us spending time together outside of work."

"Not in the Coast Guard," she shook her head. "It's my rule."

"Why?"

Tracie sighed. She'd been tired before Heath had arrived. She was exhausted now. Still, it had been so long since she'd had anyone to talk to, since she'd stood so close to anyone. She didn't want Heath to leave, so she kept talking.

"I didn't always have this rule. Before Trevor came, I wouldn't think twice about meeting a few guys from the team at the rec center for racquetball, or joining my coworkers and their families for a barbecue." She paused.

"Before Trevor came?"

"He wanted more of my attention than I wanted to give him." It took several long seconds for her to gather the courage to look Heath in the eye.

The concern on his face strengthened her, and she went on. "He thought we should hang out together. He—" she struggled to form the words she hadn't ever admitted to anyone "—he wanted to be involved with me. He thought we should get together after hours. Not that I ever would." She made a disgusted face. "I tried to turn him down politely. I tried to give him hints. When hints weren't enough I had to make myself very, very clear."

Her voice rose as the confession came spilling

out, and Gunnar lifted his head from her foot and whined his concern.

Tracie lowered her voice slightly. "I told him I didn't fraternize with coworkers. Ever. And I stuck to it. Once I thought I could get away with going to play sand volleyball with a bunch of guys from work, but he showed up. It was bad." She pinched her eyes shut against the memories. Trevor's anger. Trevor's accusations.

Heath extended his good arm, gently enfolding her shoulders. She smelled the scent of his fabric softener mixed with his aftershave, and his soft cotton shirt pulsed ever so slightly with his strong heartbeat.

"I'm sorry you had to go through that," Heath apologized. "And I'm sorry I pushed you. I didn't know."

Tracie shook her head against him, startled to find herself so close to him, but immeasurably glad for his closeness anyway. "No. Don't be sorry." She looked up into his face. "You are *nothing* like him. I don't regret letting you in tonight. I really appreciate the pizza, and the opportunity to talk."

The grin that instantly appeared on Heath's face told Tracie he didn't regret it either.

A surprised laugh burst from her lips. "If Trevor was alive right now, he would be so furious to see you here when I was so insistent on not getting involved with him."

Heath lifted her chin. "Let's just be glad he's dead, then." He looked into her eyes, his expression warm.

Returning a giddy smile, Tracie let her eyes rove over his handsome face, to his lips less than a foot from hers. What would it be like to kiss him? She was chiding herself for thinking such a thing about a man she'd only just met when Gunnar's barking protest distracted her. "Okay, Mr. Chaperone," she relented, backing away.

"I should go," Heath said, taking a step toward his coat.

The twinge of disappointment she felt took Tracie by surprise. She hadn't ever intended to have Heath over in the first place; she should have felt relieved that he was leaving. "Thanks for the pizza." She headed for the door, self-conscious about where her thoughts had roamed.

When Tracie opened the front door for Heath, Gunnar's nostrils flared and he bounded outside, barking.

"Want me to go after him?" Heath offered.

"It's okay, he usually goes out before bedtime." She bit her lower lip thoughtfully. Gunnar wasn't usually so excited about his evening ritual, but she figured Heath's visit had thrown him off his routine. Still, he barked angrily at the thorny stand of blackberry canes that rimmed the one side of her property. Strange.

"Sounds like he's pretty interested in those bushes," Heath observed. "Is that normal?"

Tracie felt her pulse tick up a notch. "Not really," she acknowledged, sliding on her oversize snow boots and tromping out at Heath's side.

"Hey, buddy." Heath went nose-to-nose with the canine. "What's up? You got a rabbit pinned in there?"

Gunnar whined at Heath, then shook his head and made a sound that may have been a sneeze, though it sounded more like the dog was disgusted about something.

"Oh!" Tracie's eyes opened wide, and she almost laughed at her dog, who could seem so human at times.

The dog turned his back on the bush and kicked snow behind him with his hind legs before trotting back to the house.

Heath escorted Tracie to the door. "You sure you're going to be okay?"

"Of course." She smiled up at him, feeling better after his visit than she had in some time.

"Call me if anything bothers you," Heath insisted. "Or if you have anything on your mind and just want to talk."

"Sure." Tracie waved as Heath trotted off to his truck.

She closed the door and locked the deadbolt after him, wondering what his final words had been about. Too tired to make any sense of it, she wandered back to the kitchen with Gunnar huffing indignantly at her feet.

Heath breathed deeply of the cold night air and tried to clear his thoughts, but his evening with Tracie had blown his mind. Sure, he'd felt attracted to her from the start, but getting to know her and taking a peek inside her world only made him want to spend more time with her and get to know her even better. Who would have guessed he'd find such an intriguing woman in this little corner of Wisconsin—and she used Gerlach Tools! It had taken all his resilience to leave her, in spite of Gunnar's insistence and his own certainty that if he went too far with Tracie too quickly, he'd push her away. She was a woman of strong convictions. He'd figured that much out already.

Nor did he think Gunnar had simply been after a rabbit in the bushes. He didn't want to scare Tracie, but he was fairly certain the ground had been recently trampled by something a lot bigger than a bunny, though whatever—or whoever—it had been was long gone. Still, Heath would be keeping a close watch on her place tonight.

And he knew one other thing for certain. Tracie had been right about Trevor. If her old partner had seen them spending time together tonight, he would be furious. From what he knew of the man, that rage would play out violently. If he was dead, of course, there was no way the issue could be a problem. But Heath was far from certain that Trevor was really dead.

FOUR

Heath met Tracie in the parking lot of the Coast Guard station when she arrived for work the next morning. He'd gone in early to talk to Jake about his plans for the day. After everything that had happened in the previous three days, Jake had been eager to agree to Heath's idea. Devil's Island was as likely a place as any for them to turn up new leads in the case. It was where Trevor's body had been discovered, then lost. If they were ever going to recover any trace of it, they'd need to do it soon—before time and wild animals took any more of a toll. And, perhaps most importantly, with a gunman loose on the mainland, Devil's Island was arguably the safest place for them to spend the day, as it was located twenty miles out on Lake Superior.

The smile Tracie flashed him as she hopped out of her car caused Heath's heart to leap and a matching expression to appear on his face. "You don't regret having me over for dinner last night?" he asked as she drew close.

"Not yet." She smirked at him, then sobered her expression. "Although our relationship remains strictly a professional one, regardless of how much time we spend with one another."

"I agree." He fell into step beside her as she headed for the building. "I talked to Jake about our plans for today."

"Plans? I've got all that paperwork—" she said, starting to protest.

He stopped walking and turned to face her. "There's a gunman on the loose and he's already taken a shot at us. I think we need to get out of Dodge, so to speak, and Jake agrees."

Tracie shook her head. "We've got a case to solve."

"And we're not going to solve it filling out paperwork like sitting ducks where anyone with evil intentions could expect to find us."

She made a squinty-eyed, thoughtful face, and Heath sensed his argument was winning her over.

"Now, the last couple leads we've tried to follow have gone cold. We need to backtrack and follow our last lead."

"Which is?" She looked at him expectantly.

"Devil's Island."

Tracie started visibly as he named the place. "Why?"

"Well, for one thing, most of the diamond smugglers' operation was centered out of the secret cave under the island. I haven't had the chance to visit it. So it's pretty high on my list of things to do. This thirty-degree weather we've been enjoying isn't going to last, either. It's supposed to snap off cold tomorrow. Even though the Bayfield crew has already searched the island, there's always the chance a new set of eyes could pick up on something they've missed. And I, for one, think it's high time we recover Trevor's body." *If it's really out there to recover,* Heath thought to himself, though he didn't say the words out loud.

"Oh. Is that all?" Tracie still looked a little uncomfortable with the idea.

"Well, there is one other thing, but I suppose it's a selfish reason."

Now her expression appeared intrigued. "What's that?"

"According to the reports I've read, Devil's Island is the place where you saved the lives of three civilians. I don't think I can fully appreciate all that you did until I've seen the place with my own eyes." Heath's voice went a little husky, and it occurred to him that Jonas would be impressed by the way his words had softened Tracie's demeanor so quickly. But Heath hadn't spoken that way to impress his boss.

Tracie blushed and dipped her head. "Well, it sounds like you and Jake have the day all worked out. It's a long trip. Let's get going."

They loaded up a utility boat with supplies. Tracie balked when Heath got out the cold-water diving gear.

"I thought we were going into the sea cave?"

"We are."

"In kayaks," she stated.

Heath shook his head. "Underwater."

"Isn't it a little late in the year for that?"

"The air temperature and surface weather patterns will have little bearing on our dive once we get under water." The way he understood it, Lake Superior had enough water mass that the surface water temperature didn't begin to dip until later in the winter, though the depths tended to hover around a temperature of forty-six degrees year-round. But Heath focused his argument on the needs of the case. "The standing assumption is that Trevor's body sank, or was sunk by his killers. If that's the case, we should be able to dive and find it—along with any other clues the diamond smugglers may have left behind." He took a step closer and softened his expression. "Your point about the season is a good one. The truth of it is, if we wait much longer, the lake will begin to ice over, and making this dive after that point would be distinctly more dangerous. I've read the weather reports. Today may be the last good day to do this."

For a moment, Tracie looked as though she might continue her protest, but then she gulped a breath and started helping him load the supplies.

Heath wondered about her response. "Do you have experience cave diving or cavern diving?" he asked.

"I've had the usual Coast Guard dive training."

Heath flinched internally. He didn't know what the usual training was, but of course, she wouldn't know that. Much as he needed to know her level of training, he didn't want to risk giving away his true identity.

Cave diving was significantly more dangerous than diving in the open sea. Not only were there often underwater currents and visibility issues, but in an emergency, ascending directly to the surface was often not possible because of the enclosed space. That made reaching oxygen vastly more difficult when every second counted. He couldn't think of a way to ask her if she recognized the added risk without revealing how little he knew of standard Coast Guard training. He'd just have to keep an eye on her. Hopefully his experience as a Navy SEAL would compensate for any lack on training as Trace's part.

The weather was especially mild for late November, and though the temperature wouldn't likely reach forty degrees, the lake was still free of ice. Heath offered to let Tracie steer.

"That's all right. I know the islands. I'd rather navigate." She had her long hair tied back in a fat twist at the nape of her neck, and a few blond strands escaped to dance against her cheeks in the brisk wind.

Once they had the boat headed toward the island, Heath had his best shot at getting Tracie to talk. Given her response when he'd mentioned her heroics the last time she'd been out to the island, he thought that might be a good topic to start with.

"I've read the report," he began, knowing her fondness for directing him back to the written version of the story, "but I'd like to hear you tell me about what happened last month on Devil's Island."

Tracie must have finally softened to him after their encounter the evening before. Jonas had been right. Now she opened up without hesitation.

"Trevor and I were called out for a search and rescue on a Saturday night almost six weeks ago. A woman named Marilyn Adams was missing out on Devil's Island. At that point we didn't know what we were dealing with. I just figured it was another case of tourists going out too late in the season, underestimating how dangerous it can be out here, and getting caught in a fast-moving storm.

"But there was a lot more to it, as you know. Diamond smugglers had been operating out of a hidden sea cave under Devil's Island, probably for at least ten years, bringing in synthetic gems through Canada. It wasn't until an expert gemologist figured it out a few months ago and reported his find in a major gemology journal that these guys decided they need to patch the leaks in their operation."

Heath nodded and kept his eyes on the helm. He knew there had actually been several reports filed on the gems over the years, but they'd never been able to follow up on them because the gemologists involved had mysteriously died shortly after their discoveries, and whatever notes or evidence they'd left behind had disappeared, leaving the FBI without anything to go on. But of course he couldn't tell Tracie that without letting her know how he'd come by the information. So he simply nodded and hoped she'd keep talking.

"Marilyn Adams had several diamonds that had originated from the smugglers, and the way I understand it, they were afraid her diamonds could be traced back to them. They cooked up a plot to bring her and her family out to Devil's Island and make their deaths looks like a collision between the remote wilderness and poor survival skills. By doing so, they also hoped to get their hands on some valuable property she owned—they needed a new source of income since their diamond gig was up.

"Are you confused yet?" Tracie pointed him around the next island.

"I think I'm following." He steered them in the direction she'd indicated. "Their plan was pretty foolproof, as I understand it. They came very close to getting away with it."

"Too close," Tracie nodded. "If Scott Frasier and Abby Caldwell hadn't managed to escape the island." Her voice caught with emotion.

Heath looked at her with sympathy. He knew she had been tied up with the others in the smuggler's hideout. She'd ultimately been the one to get help while the others fended off their captors. "And if you hadn't arrived to help them," he added.

"I was only doing my job," she insisted, her features regaining their usual stoic demeanor. "And anyway, if Trevor hadn't been involved with the smugglers, keeping the Coast Guard off their trail, I never would have become so tightly involved with the case. So you see, God can bring good things out of bad." Her words faded, as though she felt self-conscious about the faith-filled statement even before she'd finished making it.

But the integrity of Tracie's faith had only

impressed Heath, and he quickly moved to keep the conversation going. "Once the smugglers didn't need Trevor to keep us out of their hair any more, they got rid of him?"

"Pretty much. Tim thought Trevor had made some of the smugglers angry, and that may have been part of what got him killed. We suspect the head of their operation, a guy they called Captain Sal, was the one who pulled the trigger, but he won't admit to anything yet."

"Captain Sal," Heath repeated. "He's the prisoner we're transporting back to Canada tomorrow."

"Right. A lot of his crimes are under Canadian jurisdiction." She pointed to the next island in their path. "Wide to the right around this one."

Heath steered as he'd been told. "So if Sal is in custody, who's calling the shots now?"

"That's what we don't know. We thought Sal and the ten guys we captured with him were the whole group. It's hard to imagine even that many people being involved without us knowing something was going on for that long, so I can't imagine there were too many more beyond them. And though I've heard stories of criminals running their empires from behind prison walls, I don't know how Sal would have gotten his message out right under our noses."

"But if Tim was right," Heath began, taking his

eyes off the helm just long enough to look deep into Tracie's clear, blue eyes.

She nodded solemnly. "If this thing goes deeper than what we can see…" She bit her lower lip and looked concerned.

"There could be other guys out there," Heath finished for her. He launched the question he'd wanted to ask for some time. "When we were shot at Saturday, do you think we surprised somebody and they pulled a gun to keep us from stumbling on to something?"

"I wish that was it." Tracie's face pinched up in a worried expression. "But how could it be? The gunman used an AK-47 assault rifle. There wasn't a gun like that in the house. There weren't any guns in the house. John and Mack confiscated them all as evidence. To think a man would just happen to be carrying a weapon like that on him, that he'd be out there with it at the exact time we stopped by? It's absurd. He would have had to be watching out the window for us to even see us coming. The woods are thick between the road and the house. He wouldn't have had two minutes' warning even if he was watching for us."

"So you think he was expecting us?"

"How could I pretend to think otherwise?"

Heath met Tracie's eyes again and held her gaze for as long as he dared before looking back at the lake. She looked worried. No, more than that, she looked sickened by fear. "Do you have any idea who it might have been?"

"Somebody who knew when we were coming? Who knew how to get inside Trevor's house, who had a reason to take a shot at us in the first place? I wouldn't have thought such a person existed."

Her analysis made Heath's skin crawl. He wished he could drop the subject and talk about something innocent like the weather, but as Jonas had said, this was a matter of life and death. Heath had to know how close Tracie was to the inside.

"There was one guy who could have done it," he began slowly.

Tracie's eyes widened, but she didn't speak.

Heath continued. "You thought you smelled Trevor's cologne on the stoop when we arrived. Had you ever smelled it there before?"

"You mean outside?"

"Yes."

Tracie looked frightened and confused. "No, but what do you think that means? Trevor's dead."

Heath took one hand from the helm and reached for Tracie's hand. In spite of the warmth of the boat's cabin, her fingers felt cold. "Do you think there's someone else out there, wearing Trevor's cologne and Trevor's size-fourteen boots, knowing things only Trevor could have known, trying to kill us?"

"What are you trying to say?"

"Which is more likely? That somebody else is doing what only Trevor could do, or that Trevor himself took a shot at us?"

"No!" Tracie shouted, dropping his hand and backing away before he'd even finished his sentence. "Trevor is dead. I saw his body myself. I'm telling you, he's dead!"

Heath stared patiently at Tracie while he slowed the boat in preparation for reaching Devil's Island. "I know. I read the report. I know what you think you saw. But what if you're wrong? You weren't able to recover his body. It disappeared. What's more likely: that someone disposed of it that quickly, or that Trevor simply walked away?"

"Dead men don't walk away, Heath."

"True. But what if Trevor is still alive?"

Tracie stared at her new partner for a moment in fear. Was he crazy? There was no way Trevor could be alive. She had to make him understand that. They'd come around the northwest side of Devil's Island to the area of the sea caves, and she pointed up the steep brownstone cliffs to where the tops of a few wind-whipped hemlocks were just visible from below.

"Look," she pointed. "I was in the woods up there when I heard shots fired. Abby Caldwell and Scott Frasier were the first people on the scene. They saw Trevor's body in the water. I arrived seconds later, stood on that spot and looked right into this area of the lake. I saw Trevor's body floating in the water facedown."

"How can you be sure it was Trevor if he was floating facedown?"

"It *was* Trevor," Tracie insisted. "He's an unusually built guy. He was six-foot-five, really big with a distinctive body shape. Trust me, it was Trevor's body I saw. Besides that, I took blood samples from the cliff side and inside the cave. The DNA evidence came back two weeks ago. The blood belonged to Trevor. The body looked like Trevor's. You can't tell me that wasn't him."

"I believe you," Heath looked down into her eyes, and for the first time Tracie realized he had his arm around her again. Now she was glad for the support of his strong arm on her shoulder. "I believe that was Trevor who was shot, and whose body you saw. But his body was never recovered."

A chill ran down her spine. Tracie fought back the fear she felt at Heath's suggestion. "He had multiple bullet wounds. I saw them." She had to make him understand. Trevor had to be dead. The man was evil. He'd tormented her. He'd killed one of his cohorts in cold blood. If he was alive…no, he had to be dead.

"I have a bullet wound," Heath noted. "I'm not dead."

At that reminder, Tracie pinched her eyes shut.

To think that Heath could have died, just like Trevor.

"What was the nature of his wounds? Where were they located?"

"Upper torso." She closed her eyes and pictured the image that she'd never been able to exorcise from her memory. "Two wounds, maybe three. There was a lot of blood in the water."

"How high on the torso?"

"Pretty high."

"And Trevor was a big guy, right. Lots of extra bulk?"

Tracie understood what he was suggesting and pulled away from him, as though she could hide from the possibility of what his words implied. He held on to her fingertips and met her eyes.

"Is it possible the wounds could have missed major organs—that they could have been superficial muscle-tissue shots through the shoulder?"

"Yes." Tracie admitted with a shaky breath. "But he was floating facedown. *Facedown*, do you get that? You don't float facedown in Lake Superior for more than about two minutes and still live, bullet wounds or not."

"Was he in the water that long?" Heath pressed. "Do you know for a fact he was floating facedown for more than two minutes?"

And then Tracie felt it. A cold terror like she'd never felt before. Her grandmother would have said someone had walked over her grave. And maybe there was something to that. She felt as though the lid had been closed on her casket, as though her fate had been sealed. If Trevor was alive, if he was out to kill her, she didn't know how she could ever evade him. She wanted to vomit, but she slowly forced herself to look Heath in the eye. "No. I only had one look at him before we went back around the other end of the island to get the boat to retrieve his body. When we got back around to this side, he was gone."

Heath rested a tentative hand on her back, his touch so welcome after all the time she'd spent feeling isolated by Trevor. She sniffled a few times, then gave in to the tears that poured down her cheeks. Trevor. Alive. Suddenly it all made sense. He'd been the one shooting at them, he'd killed his own brother. He was after them, and Tracie knew Trevor well enough to know he wouldn't stop until he'd killed her, too.

The job she'd started to dislike when Trevor had arrived now terrified her. What had begun as a challenging occupation now seemed impossible. How could she continue to do her job with Trevor on the loose? Her only hope was to somehow bring him to justice—but that task seemed insurmountable since they knew nothing of his whereabouts, their every lead had dried up and, if they got too close to him, he'd kill them.

They needed another lead to go on, and the sea caves were their most promising option. She tipped her head up and looked into Heath's face. At his tender expression, she nearly started sobbing again out of gratitude that he was with her. But instead she blinked back her tears.

Heath cradled her face in one large hand and brushed away her tears with his thumb. "Ready to go on?"

"Yes."

She followed him dumbly as he pulled close to the island and anchored the boat. But when he pulled out the diving wetsuits, she took a deep breath and fought to stifle the fear of diving she'd worked so hard to overcome during her Coast Guard training. She thought she'd put it behind her, but now with everything else, she felt its lingering effects all the more acutely. It occurred to her that she could tell Heath about her fears, but after all the time she'd already wasted by crying on his shoulder, she knew she oughtn't bother him. It wasn't his fault her father had died making a dive in Lake Superior.

FIVE

Heath pulled on his gear inside the cramped dressing closet of the utility boat, then stepped out and waited for Tracie to finish suiting up. The same question kept circling in his mind: Was Tracie involved with the diamond smugglers? And the same answer rose like a shout in his throat: No!

But did he truly believe that, or did he keep returning to that answer because it was what he wanted to believe? Getting close to Tracie hadn't been difficult, once he'd broken through the barricade she'd put up to keep her fellow Coast Guardsmen out. But it had also proven not to be without risks. He liked Tracie, and already felt himself losing his ability to objectively evaluate her as a suspect. But he knew better than to let his feelings get in the way of the investigation.

He stepped out of the closet and saw her, suited up and ready to go, and he grinned, unable to fight back the smile that rose to his lips. Tracie Crandall was a beautiful woman. No wonder he had trouble keeping his heart from getting involved. He had already begun to hope sincerely that she hadn't been involved with the diamond smugglers. Either way, he needed to find out who was.

"Ready," she said, a look of challenge in her eyes.

"Great." He grabbed his hood. "Let's get going."

They helped each other secure their equipment, then slid into the ice-cold water. Despite their well-insulated wetsuits, Heath felt a discernable chill run straight up from his toes as he slipped into the lake. It took his eyes a moment to adjust to the reduced visibility below the swirling waters. He paddled backward to resist the surf that would have smashed him against the rocks if he let it.

Beside him, he saw Tracie gracefully flex and flow, finding a rhythm with the water, moving with it. While the wounds on his back protested, he struggled to imitate her movements, and felt a flicker of jealously at the sinuous strength in her lithe body. His brute musculature was an advantage on land, but under the force of the crashing waves where surface area was a handicap, Tracie clearly had the advantage, her slender form undulating like a frond of sea grass in the waves.

With powerful LED lights strapped to their dive hoods, they entered the sea cave. Heath looked down and was surprised to see the steep sides of the narrow passage descending infinitely below him. The bottom was beyond the reach of his light, and he wasn't ready to go looking for it. In keeping with cave diving practices, he and Tracie followed a guide line connected to the boat. That way they wouldn't become separated from one another in the darkness, or lose their way due to the disorienting influence of the pitch-black cave.

They'd discussed their strategy prior to making the dive, and now, as planned, Heath followed Tracie into the cave. She'd been inside before, albeit above water, and therefore had the greatest knowledge of the layout of the space. As the light penetrating the water grew dim, Tracie paused and gestured to the walls around them. Heath looked up and saw the opening to the movable stone door that had long disguised the interior cave, which for centuries had provided pirates and smugglers the perfect hideout right under the noses of the authorities, all but directly below the lighthouse that marked Wisconsin's northernmost point. The secret sea cave had harbored many criminals over the years behind a stone facade that opened and closed much like a garage door.

The mechanism that opened the door, though intriguing, was unlikely to yield any clues to their case, so Heath secured their guide line to mark their place, and then he and Tracie swam on toward the darkness. As all light dissipated around them, Heath instinctively pulled closer to Tracie. They proceeded forward, unreeling their guide line as they went, until they came to the rough cave walls at the far end of the enclosure. Here Heath paused, inspecting the walls closely, hoping to find some clue as to what kind of vessels had been in and out of this space recently.

Tracie bobbed along silently beside him while he scrutinized the cave walls. The variation on the color of the brownstone lent a natural camouflage to the rock walls, making it that much more difficult for Heath to detect any artificial markings. The space stretched wider than a city block, so finding anything would be like discovering the proverbial needle in a haystack. They needed to go over everything methodically; flitting from one spot to another would likely cause them to miss something.

After several minutes of searching, Tracie tugged on his sleeve and pointed downward. He looked down, noting the infinite depth of the cave. She wanted to take a look.

Heath shook his head and pointed to his wrist, trying to communicate to her that they needed to be careful of how much time they spent underwater. Though the bottom of the cave might yield some sort of clue, he wasn't ready yet to abandon his examination of the cave walls.

With a resigned look, Tracie returned her attention to examining the walls with him. Heath felt relieved. If he was honest with himself, he didn't feel completely comfortable with Tracie diving very deep in the cave. Not only did gas consumption increase with depth, but the effects of nitrogen narcosis were known to be amplified by a dive within a cave as opposed to open-water diving. Since he didn't know what kind of training Tracie had actually had, he didn't dare let her go down too deep. She could easily panic, especially if she didn't recognize the symptoms of dizziness, disorientation and exhaustion for what they were.

Heath kept close to Tracie while he searched the cave wall. They slowly made their way toward the left side of the cave, which extended under the platform the smugglers had used as a pier. Buttressed supports arched from the walls of the cave instead of straight up from the bottom. The unusual structure didn't bode well for the depth of the cave. He'd have expected the supports to lie directly beneath the platform unless the distance to the bottom was simply too great.

Next to him, he noticed Tracie inspecting a greenish-gray streak on the rock wall. He swam closer and looked over her shoulder at the stripe. The smudge was clearly not part of the natural color variation of the wall. No, deep under the pier though they were, something had scraped against the rock hard enough to leave behind residual paint.

Heath pulled his sample collection kit from the pack at his belt. Carefully, he scraped at the hard rock. Removing a sample was tricky; getting it into the bag before it floated away, even trickier. He focused all his attention on the task.

It wasn't until he'd safely zipped the sample away that he realized Tracie was missing. A quick look around the cave revealed a distant light shimmering in the depths below. Throwing all caution away, he raced downward, his only thought for her safety.

He lost track of the distance as he sped down toward her. As he brought his light into close enough range to illuminate her, he saw that she was frantically pulling up at something on the floor of the cave. For a fleeting moment, Heath wondered if she'd found the drain to the bottom of the lake, and he feared that if she pulled it out, the water would all drain away, taking them with it.

Then he quickly realized the absurdity of his thought, and recognized it for what it was: a symptom of nitrogen narcosis. And if he was feeling it, Tracie was surely already under its influence. He had to get her to the surface—if he could find the surface. With crushing fear, he realized he'd left the guide line somewhere far above them.

Already in the darkness he was having trouble distinguishing top from bottom.

Heath grabbed Tracie's arm and tried to pull her away from whatever it was she was tugging at. She pushed at him, and the frenzied look in her eyes confirmed his suspicions. He had to get her to the surface in a hurry, before the intoxicating effects of her condition caused her to do something deadly. He'd been warned in his own training about disoriented divers pulling out their own air lines, or becoming so panicked they refused to leave the bottom until their air supply ran out.

Wrapping his arms around her torso, he tried to pull her away from the heavy object that held her down. She wouldn't let go of her burden. He attempted to pry her fingers away, but when she began to fight him in earnest, he realized she wasn't leaving without it.

No, the only way to get her to leave the floor of the sea cave would be to pull them both to the surface.

Fortunately, the weight of Tracie's find made it clear which direction was down. Heath had only to resist the gravitational pull on their load to determine which way was up. The cumbersome object, about the size of a manhole cover, but thicker and tapered to a coned point, made their journey a slow one. Tracie struggled to wriggle away from him, kicking him several times.

The extra effort not only placed on additional burden on his air supply, but the extra carbon dioxide he exhaled threw off his oxygen exchange. Heath began to feel lightheaded, and strained upward to see, but no matter where he looked, there was only darkness.

He pulled against the weight and fought against the disorienting effects brought on by the lack of oxygen he was experiencing. Much as he wanted to pull them upward, he had trouble remembering which way that was. Then Heath felt a heavy blow against the wound on his arm as Tracie fought against him, and the staggering pain that ripped through him shot clarity into his mind.

He tightened his hold on Tracie and the conical chunk of metal she'd found, and propelled them upward, kicking hard with his legs. He couldn't recall where they were headed, and all but forgot what they were fighting until his head broke through the surface of the water. Tearing back his face mask, he gulped the pure, frigid air of the sea cave. Then he pulled back Tracie's mask, the beams of their lights gyrating against the ceiling until he got one twisted around so he could see Tracie's face.

Tracie's pupils contracted against the light and he watched as the frantic expression faded from her face. Together they swam below the dock to the lip of the pier, and lifted the massive steel cone through a foot or so of empty air. It grated metal against metal as they sat it on the painted steel grate of the dock.

Then Heath hoisted himself upward, and reached down to pull Tracie's slight frame up from the water. She struggled onto the platform beside him and slumped down, panting heavily. Heath's mind spun as he recalled the terror he'd felt in the dark depths, and he realized he'd nearly lost it under there. He felt a foreign sense gratitude welling up as he considered how close they had come to dying in the sea cave.

As Tracie's clarity of mind returned through a fog of confusion, she trembled from the cold and the terror of what she'd just experienced.

"Are you okay?" she asked finally, when she'd caught her breath enough to clear her thoughts.

"I think so. My arm is killing me, though. I think you might have opened up my injury."

"Your arm?" she gasped, realizing with horror that she'd fought against him underwater, though the details were blurry. She remembered how afraid she'd been that he'd bleed to death when he'd been shot. If the wound bled too profusely out here, she'd have to administer first aid and get him to help in a hurry.

"You bumped it with that—" he pointed to the

massive hunk of metal she'd pulled up from the bottom "—*thing.*"

"Evidence," she informed him, then winced at the thought of how her discovery might have re-injured the wound on his arm. "Let's get back to the boat so I can take a look at your arm."

Carrying their flippers and the unknown object they'd pulled from the bottom, Heath and Tracie clumsily walked along the length of the platform to the exit of the cave. When the ledge outside the cave ended, they had no choice but to go back in the water to swim to where they'd anchored the boat. After lugging the evidence on board, Heath got the engine and heat going, and then peeled off the top of his wetsuit so Tracie could look at his arm.

As she'd have guessed, the angry wound was weeping red. She pulled out first aid equipment and settled in to try to make up for the damage she'd caused. While she worked, the heater began to spew out warm air, and she soon felt her chattering teeth still enough to permit conversation.

"I'm sorry about what happened back there," she apologized as she pressed gauze to the antiseptic she'd daubed on his arm. "I don't know what came over me. I'm not usually like that. I wouldn't ever intentionally strike you."

"That's all right. It wasn't you."

She looked at him quizzically.

"Nitrogen narcosis," he offered.

Tracie thought she'd heard the term somewhere, but couldn't place it. "What's that?"

Closing his eyes, Heath sighed, his expression patient. "The levels of nitrogen in our air supplies weren't intended for that deep of a dive. As the depth increases, so does their concentration. They become like a narcotic. Underwater intoxication." He turned to face her and opened his eyes. "You lose your mental control, become someone else." His face held a distant look. "It's often fatal."

The gravity of their near-miss settled on her with a crushing weight. "I'm sorry. I had no idea."

"It's worse when you're diving in a cave than in open water. If I'd had any idea the cave would be that deep, I would have warned you."

"You had no way of knowing. I was shocked, and I'd been inside the cave before but not underwater. It just seemed to go down forever." Tracie finished taping the fresh bandage on his arm and closed her eyes, remembering. She'd certainly been out of it. Her thoughts had been so confused. While initially her dive had been driven by curiosity about what lay below, she'd quickly seen the flash of her light against the hunk of metal, and she'd sped down to retrieve it. Her memory muddled after that point, and she wasn't even sure what she'd been thinking when Heath reached her. She shivered.

"You should change out of that wetsuit. You'll be warmer," Heath offered.

"Good idea." Tracie hurried into the changing closet, then stepped out and took the wheel while Heath changed. The weather was unseasonably clear, and they were able to make good time through the maze of islands that separated them from the Coast Guard station in Bayfield.

With her attention focused outside, the warmth Heath's hand on her back surprised her, and she jumped. She hadn't even heard him step out.

"Sorry." Heath pulled his hand back. "Did I startle you?"

"You're okay," she reassured him, shaking off her unnecessary fear. "I'm still feeling a little jittery from that dive."

"That was rather unnerving, wasn't it?" Heath agreed.

"Dives always are," she murmured without thinking as Heath stepped past her and took over at the wheel.

"How's that?" As Heath turned and looked at her, his eyes widened, showing a desire for understanding.

Tracie immediately felt self-conscious about her unintentional revelation. "Oh, just that we never seem to dive for happy reasons. Most of the dives I've been on are to look for a body—either somebody washed overboard, or someone riding their snowmobile out onto thin ice." Her thoughts returned to the way her father had died, and she choked back an involuntary sob.

Heath kept their boat cruising toward home, but looked at her sympathetically. "Those are never easy."

"No." Tracie felt foolish. None of the guys at the Coast Guard got this emotional, certainly not around each other. She hated being different from her peers simply because she was a woman. But at the same time, her frustration only seemed to make the tears rise more readily to her eyes.

Heath slowed the boat's speed considerably.

"What are you doing?" Tracie asked. "We're almost back to Bayfield."

"I know. And you look like you need a moment." His voice broke off, and he reached for her.

Tracie took a step back, feeling mortified that he'd make any sort of special allowance on her part. "I'm okay," she insisted, quickly wiping away a tear that had sneaked past her rapidly blinking eyelids.

Withdrawing his hand, Heath nodded but didn't move the throttle. "Okay." The boat idled in the water, the lap of waves marking time as evenly as a pendulum.

Tracie almost wished Heath wasn't being so nice about her tears. Trevor would have made some nasty remark that would have irked her enough to bury her sadness with anger. But Heath's silent kindness warmed a part of her heart that had been cold for so long she'd lost all feeling there. Now it ached with thawing sadness.

His fingertips brushed her hand.

She looked up into his compassionate eyes and realized she couldn't hide her emotions from him. "I hate diving," she confessed in a strained whisper.

Heath took hold of her hand. "I wish I'd known that. I wouldn't have asked you to go."

"It's not your fault." She took a shaky breath. He might as well know. If he knew, at least he'd realize she had some reason for being extra sensitive. "It's my dad's." Her swollen throat cut short her words.

The lapping waves rocked them gently, their nudging motion prompting her to slowly open her heart and trust Heath with the terrors of her past.

"Did your father teach you to dive?" Heath asked after an extended silence.

Tracie shook her head and struggled to speak. "No. He was going to. He never got the chance. He died making a dive in Lake Superior."

Heath closed his eyes and pressed her hand to his lips while the boat bobbed in the open water. "I'm sorry," he said simply, his lips brushing her hand.

Feeling as though a weight greater than that of

the steel cone they'd hefted from the seabed had been lifted from her, Tracie sniffed and said, "So am I."

She fell silent again, and Heath put the boat into gear, pointing them back toward the mainland. He gradually increased their speed until they reached the cruising speed of eighteen knots. "How did it happen?" he asked after another silence.

"He was in the Coast Guard, stationed in Bayfield." Tracie found her voice worked much better now that she'd regained most of her composure. Speaking helped to work out the rest. "They had a call, a submarine of all things, in distress. There were four men on board. My father pulled all four of them to safety, but then, somehow, my father drowned. I'd hoped by joining the Coast Guard I could learn more about what happened, but no one seems to know anything."

"How long ago did it happen?"

"Fourteen years ago this summer."

"That's a long time," Heath acknowledged. "What about the four men he rescued?"

"One's dead now. I've traced two of them to Canada, but the trail ends there, and the other may as well have never existed for all I've managed to find out about him. So I guess I'll never know what happened, or why there was a submarine on this lake in the first place."

Heath went silent.

Tracie wondered if she'd made him uncomfortable with her emotional confession and the memories of her father.

But then he spoke up. "Submarines aren't very common up here, are they?"

"Pretty much unheard of. Why?"

Heath stared back out at the lake, steering them past Basswood Island on the final stretch of the journey toward home.

"Why do you ask?" Tracie prodded after some silence.

He glanced back at the chunk of metal they'd retrieved from the bottom of the sea cave. His face looked pained. "Do you know what that thing is you dragged out of the lake?"

"No idea. You?"

"It's part of a submarine."

"No," Tracie protested immediately, his revelation cutting too close. "That doesn't make any sense. How would it have gotten inside the cave? That's—that's absurd. How do you even know what it is?"

Heath kept one hand on the steering wheel while he picked up the large hunk of metal with his other hand. "It's a conning cap. It goes on the end of the mast, on the sub's conning tower. When submarines want to surface through ice, they use the point of this—" he rapped on the blunted tip with his fingers "—to poke through the ice."

Tracie had seen photos of submarines surfaced at the North Pole before; she'd just never thought much about how they got up through the thick ice. "And how did it get inside the cave?"

"I suppose a sub went into the cave, started poking up through the ice, and the conning cap got knocked off—possibly by hitting the roof of the cave. Subs don't usually surface through ice in an enclosed space, so the cap wouldn't have been built to withstand anything harder than ice."

Tracie shook her head, pushing away the idea, which seemed too far-fetched, too fantastical to have taken place so close to home. "You think a submarine went *inside* the Devil's Island sea cave? That whole cave can't be more than about three hundred feet long. Look at your Ohio class subs— they're over five hundred feet long. They wouldn't even begin to fit, let alone maneuver in there."

A smirk spread across Heath's lips. "You just happen to know off the top of your head how long an Ohio class sub is, huh?"

"I did a lot of research on submarines after my dad died in one," she explained defensively, though she found his expression appealing, and suddenly had to fight back the attraction she felt toward him.

Heath sobered at the mention on her father's death. "Then you know not all subs are that long.

The more common size is in the two-fifty- to four-hundred-foot range."

"That's still way too big to get inside the cave, let alone maneuver."

"What about a midget sub?"

"Like the shark class?"

"Sure. They're about fifty feet long, have a crew of four." He stopped suddenly and met her eyes.

Tracie understood why. "Four men. Just like the submarine my dad died in."

"Do you know what kind it was?"

"No. The only ones who ever saw it were the four guys he rescued, my dad and his partner. They went out during a storm and the waters were too stirred up to see the vessel clearly. When the Coast Guard went back out later, the submarine was gone."

"Gone where?" Heath nosed the boat toward the Coast Guard dock.

"Apparently the guys came back out and got it unstuck. It wasn't in very deep water. They'd run aground on the Devil's Island shoals less than a mile east of Devil's Island. The sea depth goes from the eighty- to one-hundred-foot range, to suddenly less than thirty feet deep, which is probably why they ran aground in the first place."

"So it could still be somewhere in these waters," Heath clarified. "It could come and go from inside the Devil's Island sea cave."

Tracie's looked out at the blue-gray waves all around them, wondering what might be lurking just beneath. Was the submarine her father died in still active in the lake? Her heart beat so loudly she could hardly hear Heath. She'd searched so long and hard for clues to her father's death, but she'd given up on ever learning what really happened to him. The submarine he'd died in had disappeared as though it had never existed, along with the four men he'd saved. And now, after fourteen years, she'd dragged a clue up from the watery depths.

She looked at Heath. His gaze didn't leave hers.

"Don't forget to watch where we're going," she reminded him finally.

He glanced up through the windshield, then back at her. "You don't think—" he began.

Tracie fought back the strange creeping sensation that had been climbing up her spine. "No." She shook her head, and spoke with as much certainty as she could muster. "No, that was fourteen years ago. I'm sure it was damaged when it ran aground, or surely it's been wrecked since. And anyway, the odds alone are ridiculous."

Then she took several deep breaths and tried to convince herself that the submarine her father had died on wasn't being used to smuggle diamonds in Lake Superior.

SIX

Heath felt nervous as he drove up the road to Tracie's house with a box of fried chicken and biscuits on the seat beside him. Though he'd called ahead and she was expecting him, and she'd even sounded pleased to hear his supper plans, Heath still wasn't sure how wise it was to spend so much time alone with her.

The connection between them was strong enough already, especially after the emotional conversation they'd shared on the boat ride home. It wouldn't be easy for him to get over her when all of this was over and they went their separate ways, and if he felt that way, knowing going into it that it wouldn't last, he couldn't imagine how much the truth would hurt her. If it had been up to him, he'd back off.

But it wasn't up to him. Jonas wanted him on Tracie like a fly on butter, or so he'd insisted when Heath had called him earlier. Though Heath wanted to believe Tracie had nothing to do with the diamond smugglers, he still couldn't prove it, and anyone who wanted to question his objectivity would have plenty of reason to do so if they knew how much he'd begun to care for her. He hoped to learn enough tonight to prove she hadn't been involved with Trevor and the diamond smugglers. But he knew there was still a possibility what he learned could indicate the opposite, especially given the arguable likelihood she still harbored some level of resentment toward the Coast Guard for her father's death.

Heath parked his truck and grabbed the food and his awkwardly wrapped parcel. If nothing else, he needed to see Tracie tonight so he could give her the gift he'd bought for her.

"Come on in," she greeted him with a smile, holding Gunnar back by the collar as the large dog attempted to welcome Heath affectionately.

"Where can I put the chicken so he doesn't get to it?"

"I've got the oven set on warm. We can throw it in there. I found some information online that I want to show you." She released the dog as they headed toward the kitchen.

Heath obediently set the oven-safe box inside the warm oven, then turned to her with the present behind his back. "I brought you something. Or did you want to show me what you found online first?"

"It can wait. You've got my curiosity up." She looked up at him expectantly. Her hair was still wet and slicked back into a loose braid that hung halfway down her back. Her face looked fresh and free of makeup, though her pink lips shimmered with something that made them look irresistible.

"Close your eyes." Heath said softly, taking just a moment to relish the expectant, innocent expression on her face before he placed his gift in her outstretched hands.

Snapping her eyes open and peeling back his impromptu wrapping job, Tracie gave a happy shout.

"I take it you know what it is?"

The gratitude shining in her eyes told him she both recognized and appreciated the extra-small-sized steel-plated body armor. "How did you know I've wanted one of these since Saturday?"

"I didn't know," He confessed, setting the body armor, wrapping paper and all, on the table behind them. His voice grew gruff. "I wanted you to have one. I don't want to lose you."

Though he reached for her and longed to pull her into his arms, it still surprised him when she wrapped her arms around him and gave him a grateful hug.

"Gentle now," he suggested as her sudden squeeze made his bruises ache.

Tracie pulled away immediately. "I'm sorry." She looked slightly disoriented for a moment.

Not wanting her to become embarrassed by her sudden burst of affection, Heath quickly changed the subject. "What did you find online?" he prompted her.

"I did a little research on shark class subs," she pulled him toward the living room where her laptop lay open to a page on naval history.

"The shark class midget nuclear subs—" she took a shaky breath and began to read the article "—were built in the 1980s for speed and maneuverability, and could actually be lifted up out of the water and carried by train or truck when needed. They were all named after different kinds of sharks. During the Gulf War, two of them were lost with all hands: the *Bramble* and the *Requiem*. The *Bramble* was later found and raised, and her sailors were given a proper burial, but the *Requiem* was never located." She met Heath's eyes. "It disappeared, along with all four men inside."

Though he didn't often give in to feelings of fear, Heath felt a distinct creeping sensation as the fine hairs on the back of his neck stood up in response to Tracie's words. He watched silently as she opened another window to an article about the *Requiem* and continued reading.

"In 1990, the *Requiem* was engaged in an offensive operation as part of the Gulf War, and disappeared without a trace with all four hands on board. Efforts to locate the wreck have proven unsuccessful, as the area in which she was lost is one of many strong currents, and the sub may have drifted hundreds or even thousands of miles from the point where contact was initially lost." Tracie stopped reading and turned her head to face Heath.

"'May have drifted thousands of miles,'" he repeated, then added his own ending: "or been driven." He reached around her for the touchpad mouse and toggled the screen up and down. "Does it give the names of the men who were on her?"

"No. I couldn't find that information anywhere online."

"I may have some contacts in the Navy who can help us out." He draped a comforting arm around her shoulder. "I think we're on to something."

"But what? Is there any way of proving that conning cap came from the *Requiem*?"

"I don't think so, not without having the rest of the ship to match it to." Heath had looked the piece over very carefully once they'd returned to shore. "There's no serial number on the portion we retrieved, and even if there were, it doesn't prove the sub is actually in Lake Superior. The cap may have been transported here and dropped, which is probably just as likely as the possibility of the entire sub making its way here."

Tracie massaged her forehead with her fingertips. "There are so many possibilities it makes my head spin."

"Don't think about it for a while," Heath suggested. "We should eat, don't you think?"

"Excellent idea." Tracie led him back into the kitchen. Unlike the night before when they'd eaten the pizza right out of the box, tonight she'd set the table, complete with linen napkins and a cheery vase of artificial flowers as centerpiece.

While Tracie grabbed honey, jam and butter, Heath retrieved the food he'd brought from the oven.

Tracie poured large glasses of milk for both of them. "Everything's ready. Do you want to say the blessing?" She sat and looked at him expectantly over her folded hands.

Heath slowly lowered himself into his chair, frantically trying to think, his usually astute mind blank. The only table blessing he could think of was his goofy uncle's *good bread, good meat, good God, let's eat.* He was pretty sure Tracie wouldn't appreciate that one. He felt equally certain that any attempt he might make at an impromptu prayer would quickly give away how long it had been since he'd talked to God. "I, um—" he started, folding his hands, pulling them apart, folding them again.

"It's okay." She placed a calm hand over his nervous fingers. "I can bless it."

They both bowed their heads, and Tracie said a few simple lines of thanks.

At her amen, he looked up, about to apologize again.

Tracie beat him to it. "Sorry to put you on the spot like that."

"No, it's okay," he assured her. "I just wasn't really thinking along those lines." They hadn't bothered to bless their pizza the night before, but he should have realized that by now Tracie was comfortable enough around him to share the more intimate things in her life—like her relationship with God. Jonas's plan assumed she'd open up to him once he got close to her. The fact that she'd openly prayed with him was just another indication of how close the two of them were becoming.

"Mmm, chicken," Tracie smiled up at him as she selected a piece for herself. "Thanks so much for supper."

"No problem. We needed some comfort food after the day we've had." He took a piece for himself and watched Tracie drizzle honey on a biscuit. There was so much information he still needed to learn from her, but getting her to talk would be a delicate process. She'd already told him so much. If he made her suspicious he might not learn anything, and that wouldn't help either one of them. More than anything, he wished she'd reveal something that would prove her innocence, so he could convince Jonas to let him tell her his true identity.

But coming right out and asking her would no doubt backfire completely. Heath thought back to the psychology class he'd taken years before, recalling the innate way people internally kept track of how much they'd shared about themselves. People tended to try to keep their self-revelation interpersonally fair, if only on a subconscious level. Which meant if Heath expected Tracie to share any more of her life, he needed to share a little of his. "Fried chicken reminds me of Sunday dinners at my grandparents' house," he offered, taking a bite of biscuit and watching her expectantly.

Tracie smiled at him and silently munched her chicken.

Perhaps he'd need to share a little more than that before she opened up. "We used to go over to my grandparents' every Sunday after church." If nothing else, Heath at least hoped to win some points by mentioning church.

"Do you see your family often?" Tracie asked.

Her question required some thought. Heath didn't mind talking about things from his distant child-hood, but he didn't want to reveal too much about his recent life, which didn't match the story she'd been told. He couldn't afford to blow his cover until he was certain she wasn't involved with the diamond smugglers. "Since I joined the military I tend to see them once a year," Heath confessed. He'd joined the Navy SEALs right out of college. Tracie knew that much. From there he'd gone on to the FBI, but his cover said he'd transferred to the Coast Guard. "It's difficult to make it home."

"How many years has that been?"

He did the math quickly in his head. "Twelve."

Concern filled her features. "Don't you miss them?"

"Sometimes," Heath warred against his instinctive wish for privacy that made him want to change the subject, to hide his true feelings. He knew he needed to share part of himself with Tracie before he could expect her to tell him more of her story. She'd told him about losing her father, and that was something he doubted many people knew. Which meant he was already beholden to her. He dredged up the pain of the long-buried past and laid it out in front of her.

"I miss not having a relationship with my family," he confessed, picking at the remainder of his chicken. "My parents were always at work when I was growing up. Work during the day, work-related functions at night, or just too exhausted from it all to spend time with me. My life was spent with a series of babysitters. Sunday dinners were the closest I came to really feeling like I belonged, like I had a family at all." He looked up and met her eyes. "I guess I can't say I really miss them. I didn't ever know them that well. But I miss not ever knowing them."

The way Tracie's face shone with compassion made Heath feel awful. True, he'd had a lonely childhood and had always wished his parents would have cared more about him. But it didn't seem fair to Tracie that he should use his past to manipulate her.

"Is it too late to go back?"

Heath swallowed a bite of biscuit. "They want me to. My parents want to retire, to pass the family business on to the next generation. But I don't want to be like them. I spent my whole childhood resenting the family business. How could I go back there?"

"When my dad died—" Tracie began, then blushed and looked down.

"What?" Heath encouraged her gently.

"No, it's nothing. I don't want to sound like I'm trying to lecture you. I'm sure I can't understand what it was like for you, growing up with such distant parents."

"No, please. Tell me. I want to know what you're thinking."

Hope sparkled in her eyes when she looked up at

him. "When my dad died, I wanted to understand what had happened. Not just how he died, but why he loved Lake Superior so much, why he loved the Coast Guard. When I walk into work, I wonder how he felt, walking through the same door, with the same mission I have. I know he loved his job. I just—" She pinched her eyes shut.

Heath leaned forward and took her hand. "You what?"

"I want to love it, like he did. But I don't. I thought it would be an adventure, that it would draw me closer to my dad. But right now it seems like it's out to kill me, too. Is that how I'm supposed to get close to him?" The tears that had been welling up in her eyes spilled over, and she shoved them away with her open palms. "I'm sorry. I'm sorry I keep crying in front of you. I'm not usually a weepy person."

"Under the circumstances, I think it's more than understandable."

Tracie shook her head. She stood and turned away toward the sink.

Heath rose and wrapped his arms around her, discovering she fit perfectly in his arms. As if she was meant to be there. "Hey," he said after a moment's silence.

She tilted her head back and looked him in the face.

"I'm not going to let them get you. I saved

you on Saturday, I can do it again. You're safe with me."

"But what if you're not there?"

"I will be." Heath felt his parents' absence acutely, the dredged-up memories of his lonely childhood fresh and raw in his promise. He knew he could do better. He had to. "I will be there to keep you safe."

Tracie trembled in his arms as she pulled back. For a moment he thought she was going to step away, and he felt disappointment at the thought. Instead, she turned to hug him back. They stood in a solid embrace for several long moments before Tracie broke away. "I need to feed Gunnar."

While Tracie took care of her dog, Heath cleaned off the table and rinsed their glasses at the sink. Then he padded into her living room, where the dying embers of a fire burned low in her wood stove. Heath busied himself stoking the fire. By the time Tracie found him he had a cheery blaze going.

"Oh," she sighed as she stepped to his side in front of the fire. "Thank you. It was getting a little chilly in here."

He would have loved to wrap his arms around her again, but he didn't want to scare her away. She'd already placed so much trust in him—trust he knew he hadn't really earned, since he was pushing her to open up to further his investigation.

Besides, he knew they needed to keep talking. Jonas wouldn't be nearly satisfied with what he'd learned so far tonight. And with a killer on the loose, they needed information—fast. But Tracie was proving to be a complex woman. Heath knew he'd have to be careful, especially after all she'd shared with him so far. Fortunately, she spared him the work of finding an opening line.

"Could I ask a favor of you?" she asked in a tentative voice.

"Of course."

"Could we pray together? I just feel so overwhelmed by all of this, but I know God is in charge. He can handle it, if I can just figure out how to let Him."

Her words seemed to suck all the air from the room. Heath wasn't sure how to respond. So far, he'd knowingly misled her, but he hadn't had to fake the attraction he felt toward her. Faking a relationship with God was something else entirely. Mission or not, he didn't know how he could do it. Surely she'd understand if he told her the truth?

"I don't—" he hesitated. What if she hated him? No, he had to trust her. He had to be honest about that much, at least. "I don't really pray."

Cold air swept in to fill the void as Tracie took a step back and looked up at him. The warmth that had grown in her eyes all evening now faded, replaced by a distant, distrustful expression. No, Tracie didn't hate him. She was afraid of him.

As Tracie stared at Heath, she had to remind herself that she didn't really know him. He'd arrived in Bayfield on Thursday. Today was Tuesday. They'd known each other six days, and she'd grown impossibly close to him in that short time period. But she didn't know him—obviously not. How could she have just assumed that because he'd gone to church on Sunday, because he'd said he'd gone to church as a child, that somehow made him a Christian? She needed to be more careful.

"I'm sorry. I just assumed—"

"No, *I'm* sorry. That came out all wrong. It's not that I don't believe in God." He started to raise his hands in a hopeless gesture, then flinched and grabbed his injured arm.

"Oh, no." she led him to the couch. "Do you need an ice pack for that?"

"It'll be okay," he said through clenched teeth.

"I'm getting an ice pack," she said, already halfway to the kitchen.

"You don't have to. I'll be fine," he called after her, but the pain in his voice belied his words.

Tracie hurried back and sat close on the couch beside him, pressing the ice pack to his wound and shushing his protests. "You've got to take care of yourself," she chided him. "You're supposed to protect me, remember? How can you do that if you're too injured to be of any use?"

He didn't answer her question, but looked her straight in the eye. "I do believe in God, Tracie. I want you to understand that. I grew up in the church. I know there's a God out there, somewhere, and I'd like to believe we're working for the same team."

She cringed internally at the words *out there* and *somewhere*. For her, God wasn't *out there*. He was in her heart, closer than any person. She wished Heath could understand that, but she wasn't sure how to explain it to him without pushing him farther away. She prayed silently for guidance. "How can you work together if you never talk?"

A light seemed to come on in Heath's eyes, but he said nothing, so she continued. "Prayer is talking to God, it's reporting for duty. It's like God is Jake, and the Bible is our field manual."

Heath's eyes crinkled at the corners. "I think you've just given Jake a tremendous promotion."

"It's an analogy." She smiled back, then sobered. "I'm glad you believe in God. I wish you knew Him personally." She'd assumed he had, or she wouldn't have allowed herself to fall for him. Now it tore at her heart to know she was starting to care for a man whom she couldn't have a future with. Her faith was central to her life. Any man who wanted to be romantically involved with her would have to feel the same way.

Heath readjusted the ice pack on his arm with a thoughtful expression before he said, "I guess I just never understood the point."

"Of prayer?" she clarified.

He sighed. "Yeah. Think about it—God loves us, right?"

"Yes."

"And so He wants what's best for us?"

"Of course." Tracie wondered where he was going with his line of questioning.

"So why do we have to ask? Why doesn't God just automatically do what's in our best interest? How could our asking ever change His will?"

Tracie leaned back and looked deep into Heath's eyes. Sincere struggle shined back at her. And she couldn't think of an answer. "I don't know." She exhaled a defeated sigh and tried to think of some explanation. She knew deep in her heart there had to be one, but her mind drew a complete blank. Looking around the room as if for answers, her eyes rested on the clock. Five minutes to seven. She squinted. There was something significant about that time. Something she was supposed to be doing.

Suddenly she leapt off the couch and ran for her shoes. "I've got to go!"

SEVEN

"Go where?" Heath asked, leaping up and following her to where he'd left his boots.

"Class. I've got class in five minutes at the Bayfield rec center." She pulled on her parka and started patting the many pockets. "Keys. Where are my keys?"

Heath pulled his out his own keychain. "I'll drive. I've got you blocked in anyway."

With an authoritative nod, Tracie agreed and leapt for the door. "We have to hurry."

She goaded him on for the entire short trip back into Bayfield, directing him to the quickest route and fretting about the falling snow until they reached the looming wooden activity center at the foot of the bluff just a couple of blocks from the Coast Guard station. He barely had his truck in park before she opened her door and leapt out.

"Am I welcome?" he asked, following her inside.

She cast one of her trademark gorgeous smiles over her shoulder. "Of course."

Heath felt himself grinning as he followed her. He had no idea what this class was she had led him to, but he found the mini-mystery just as intriguing as the woman in front of him, and just another part of her allure. Then he entered the gymnasium and stopped short.

The large open space was filled with women, many of them at least seventy years old. With so many venerable ladies in the crowd, Heath wondered which one of them would be teaching the class. He hung back along the wall and watched with interest.

Tracie peeled off her coat and addressed the crowd. "Sorry I'm late. Shall we get started with our stretching? All right, line up."

As Heath watched, not just a little bit surprised, the women in brightly-colored sweatsuits formed ranks facing Tracie. Before his eyes, she led them through a series of stretches, leading up to a slow-motion routine of kicks and thrusts. It took Heath a few minutes to figure out exactly what was going on, but when Tracie starting instructing the ladies on eye-jabs and kicks to the knee, neck and groin, he realized she was teaching them self-defense kickboxing.

The room rang out with synchronized grunts as Heath watched, impressed, while Tracie ran the ladies through their drills. Then she had them pair up and pretend to attack each other.

"Remember," Tracie called out above the clamor, "you never want to place yourself in a position where you have to use these moves. Avoid dangerous situations. If you have the opportunity, run away. But if it comes down to your life or your attacker's, do not be a victim. You have the knowledge. You have the ability to defend yourself."

The hour sped by quickly as Heath watched the ladies work through their exercises. As the minute hand moved closer to the twelve, the women began to cajole Tracie.

"Will you do a bag routine for us tonight?"

"Show us those high kicks you do."

"You got here late, so you can stay late, can't you?"

Their good-natured tones, as well as Tracie's reluctant smiles, told Heath she'd probably give in, as he guessed she did often.

But Tracie shook her head. "Really ladies, this is about you, not me."

"I know what it is," a stout woman in a purple sweatsuit declared. "She doesn't want to do a routine in front of her boyfriend."

That wiped the smile from Tracie's face. "He's not my boyfriend," she denied, her face red. "He's my partner."

Heath was surprised at how much her public

rejection stung, and he realized he'd begun to think of her as something more. But he quickly chastised himself for feeling that way. He wasn't going to be in her life for very long. It was better that she not think about him in close terms.

The same purple-suited woman chided her. "You young folks and your political correctness. Partner!" she harrumphed.

"He's my *Coast Guard* partner," Tracie clarified.

"Well, maybe he'd like to do the drill with you," another woman suggested, and several others agreed emphatically.

Heath couldn't hold back the grin that spread across his face. He straightened and slowly approached Tracie.

She watched him with wide eyes. "No. I don't think that would be wise. I mean, he's injured, for one thing. And he hasn't signed the participant's waiver."

"Oh, you know that's just so none of us will sue you if we get hurt," the purple-suited woman called out. "He's not going to get hurt."

"I wouldn't be so sure about that," another woman reprimanded her.

Heath strode closer to Tracie, trying to make up his mind how to stage his attack.

She shook her head at him as he approached.

"No, Heath," she warned him. "You're injured. Not a good idea."

He met her eyes and tried to see into her soul. Was she really afraid of him? If she was, he wouldn't push it. He'd walk away, and bear the brunt of the booing from the ladies that was sure to follow. "So don't hit me on my arm," he said simply.

Her expression formed a half smirk. She was considering it. No, she wanted to, though her fear of hurting him was holding her back. He didn't care if he got hurt. He was more than curious to see what she could do. He took one final step closer, telling himself that if she turned him down again, he'd walk away.

But before that exchange could take place, she surprised him with a swift roundhouse kick to his ribs, followed at blinding speed by a back kick in his calf, which knocked his foot out from under him, sending him down on one knee.

As the ladies watching erupted with applause, Tracie took a bow.

"Thank you," she answered jovially. "That concludes your demonstration."

Feeling inspired, Heath hopped up behind her and wrapped one arm around her shoulders. He almost smiled when her elbow flew back and her open palm caught him underneath the chin. She was good—fast, powerful and so sly he had yet to anticipate a single move before she hit him. Impressive.

The ladies cheered as Tracie swept his feet out from under him and he went down a second time.

"Okay," he said, standing, "now that I know what you can do, I think I'll have to fight back."

"Heath," Tracie shook her head at him, but she was grinning openly now, and easily blocked the jabs he sent her way. He wished he didn't have to worry about his arm. They could have had a lot of fun together otherwise.

As it was, they sparred for another full minute before Heath finally managed to knock Tracie off her feet. When he offered her a hand up, it didn't occur to him that she might try to pull him down until he was lying flat the mat beside her.

The ladies hooted and hollered, and Heath recognized the voice that chided sarcastically, "*Partners,* right."

Tracie laughed as she rolled onto her side, but she asked in a serious tone, "I didn't hurt you, did I?"

"I keep trying to tell you I'm invincible. I don't know why you don't believe me." He rose and kept a watchful eye on her as she ended the class, until she had her coat on and was headed out of the building at his side. "That was fun," he said as they stepped into the chill of the night air.

"Yeah. I needed a break." Tracie stopped still and looked up into the frantic snow that swirled from the sky all around them. The cold front had moved in with a vengeance, and had already dumped a couple of inches of snow on the ground since they'd been inside.

"Nice weather," he noted, stopping beside her and blinking into the blizzard.

"Not bad."

"Think Jake will postpone Sal's transfer tomorrow?"

"I don't know. He's moved it twice already."

"I wish he would," Heath confessed. "After what we found today, I'd like a shot at questioning Sal about the submarine."

Tracie said nothing, but sighed and headed for the passenger side of his truck. He opened her door for her before climbing in the other side and driving into the blizzard in silence. "What's on your mind?"

"Hmm?" She gave him a distant look.

"Something's troubling you."

He sensed Tracie squirming on the seat beside him, but he kept his eyes on the road. Between the darkness and the blinding snow, he didn't dare look away, even for a moment. He slowed the vehicle to a crawl, unable to see the lines on the road.

"You are so different from Trevor," she observed in a wistful voice.

"That a good thing?"

She made a sound that was half laughter, half derisive snort. "In every way good. Trevor would never have noticed if something was bothering me. Or if he did, he'd accuse me of being a moody female."

Heath had heard enough from Tracie to suspect her dislike for her partner went deeper than his lack of sensitivity. "That wasn't the worst of it, was it?"

The swallowing sound in her throat was audible, her voice barely so. "Not by a long shot."

"Care to tell me?"

"I don't complain."

"It wouldn't be complaining."

She sat silently for so long, Heath feared she wasn't going to continue their conversation at all. He nudged her gently. "Tracie, if Trevor really is alive, and if he's the one who took a shot at us the other day, I'd feel a whole lot more comfortable if I knew what threats he might have made against you in the past. Because if he decided to act on one, we'd have a lot better chance of pulling through if we both had an idea of what to expect."

"Good point," she acknowledged, though she still sat in silence as they crawled down the road for another couple of minutes. Finally she offered, "I learned self-defense because of Trevor."

"To protect yourself from him?"

"Yes."

"That bad, huh?"

"He was pretty upset when I rejected him. He kept trying to get me alone after that, where there weren't witnesses. When we had to be alone, I kept my hand on my radio and made sure he knew it. That didn't stop him from trying whatever he could get away with. As long as he figured I couldn't prove it, he'd try it. Of course, he was always perfect whenever anyone else was around."

Heath felt her fear and humiliation and wished he could go back in time and protect her. His fingers tightened around the steering wheel. "Why didn't you report him? Ask to be paired with someone else?"

"Would that have stopped him?" Tracie asked. "In my experience, making him angry only made things worse—he'd become more determined, more insidious. Besides, I'm not a quitter. I don't expect special treatment just because I'm a woman."

"But he only harassed you because you're a woman," Heath reminded her, frustrated that she'd had no escape from Trevor's ongoing abuse.

"It's not as though I did nothing," Tracie reminded him. "I learned self-defense. And you can believe if he'd tried anything when there were witnesses, I'd have reported him immediately. But he made sure it never would have been anything except his word against mine. He's cruel, but he's not stupid."

"Did you ever use your moves on him?"

"Not really," she shrugged. "It helped to know how to be quick and evasive, but that's it. I think about him sometimes when I run through a drill, about how I would defend myself from him, but I wonder if I'd have the guts to do it in a real-life situation."

"I hope you never have to find out." Her failure to remind him of Trevor's supposed death didn't elude his attention. She'd apparently come to grips with the possibility. Heath was glad for that. If she *did* have to face the man, knowing ahead of time he was still around would make the experience slightly less traumatic.

They reached Tracie's house through the blinding snow. Heath wished it had been a longer trip so he'd have had an excuse to keep her talking. But since he had to drive back through the blizzard to get back to his apartment in Bayfield, he knew he didn't dare stick around much longer. Both of them were tired.

With the vehicle in park, he took Tracie's hand and met her eyes. "I'm sorry you had such an awful experience with Trevor. It makes me appreciate what a chance you took trusting me."

"I had to believe not all partners are awful."

"Can I walk you to your door?"

"I think I can make it. You've got a long trip ahead of you." She gave his hand a slight squeeze before dropping it and hopping out of the truck. Heath watched Gunnar come barreling through the doggie door to greet her as she approached the house.

Loneliness swept over him as he watched Tracie play with the dog a moment before unlocking her front door and letting them in. She hadn't even wished him good-night.

Heath knelt beside his bed and folded his hands, a position he hadn't assumed in over twenty years. But he'd decided since his conversation with Tracie that he was going to pray, and all his memories of what his nannies had taught him included kneeling to say his bedtime prayers.

"Dear God," he began, feeling self-conscious and awkward. "Heath here. I know it's been a while since I checked in, but there's a killer on the loose, after us. And I don't know..." He sighed, feeling a thousand times more foolish already. Was God even listening to him?

He felt just as he had as a child, knocking tentatively on his father's office door, waiting for a gruff "come in," before daring to turn the knob and make his request. So often, his father hadn't even looked up from whatever he'd been working on. "Ask your mother," he'd told him so many times, and Heath had gone to her, only to have her say, "Aren't you a big boy now? Can't you do that yourself?"

The lesson had been deeply ingrained. If he wanted anything, it was up to him. His parents worked hard to keep a roof over his shoulders and food on the table. Surely God was much the same, hard at work running the universe, too busy to be bothered by Heath's concerns.

He hopped into bed and stared at the ceiling. "I want to know You," he whispered into the dark.

But there was no answer, and he soon fell asleep.

Standing outside the Coast Guard station the next morning, Heath flexed his fingers in frustration, wishing he could be alone with the prisoner long enough to ask him about the submarine. Though Captain Sal had been questioned several times during his incarceration, he'd refused to reveal anything about his involvement in the diamond-smuggling ring, or even whether he'd been the one to shoot Trevor. But without evidence, a confession, or even a body, Sal couldn't be charged with Trevor's murder. Since he was wanted in Canada on several greater charges, he was being transferred. They'd have to cut through a lot of red tape before Heath could again come so close to talking to him.

Heath and Tracie stood by while the Canadians finished making preparations for the transfer of the prisoner. They weren't even to be allowed any contact with him, but were merely standing by to make sure the transfer of the high-profile criminal went smoothly.

"There's our man," Tracie whispered as a door opened on the sheriff's vehicle and two deputies stood on either side of Sal as he rose, his arms handcuffed in front of him.

Heath watched as his last bid for the truth stepped doggedly toward the pier and the boat that would take him out of their reach. The deputies stepped back as Sal mounted the steps to the boat.

Thwack! Thwack!

The sound of bullets hitting flesh took Heath by surprise. A splash of red streaked the Canadian vessel and Sal reeled forward.

"Man down!" someone shouted.

Heath tried to guess the trajectory of the bullets, frantically searching for the gunman. Chaos erupted around them as men dived for cover. If Sal was fatally hit, as Heath was certain he had been, then there would be no future opportunity to question him. His only shot at the truth would be if he could wrangle a deathbed confession from him, much as Tim had whispered Trevor's name before he died.

Heath crouched down and stepped toward the boat.

Thwump!

Tracie let out a startled groan as she went down behind him.

"Tracie!" Heath screamed, turning back to her. She was hit. He forgot all about Sal and scooped her up from where she'd fallen hard on the cement. A desperate feeling overtook him as he realized he might lose her.

She blinked up at him. "He's on the roof of the museum." Her voice sounded weak as she lifted one hand and pointed toward the maritime museum half a block away.

"The roof of the museum!" Heath shouted, looking where she pointed and seeing the flash of a dark figure ducking away. "The gunman's on the museum roof! Don't let him get away!"

Officers scrambled everywhere, some clustered where Captain Sal had fallen, others heading for their vehicles while a few took off on foot in the direction he had pointed. The pandemonium faded to the background as Heath focused all his attention on Tracie. He still wasn't sure how badly she'd been hit. His heart clenched and he felt as though he couldn't breathe. Though he'd seen a lot of injuries during his years of service, none scared him as much as Tracie's.

"Go get him," Tracie insisted, her rasping voice

gaining strength as she struggled for breath. "I'm fine. Go after him."

"I'm not going to leave you."

Her eyes hardened, boring into his. "It's Trevor."

"I don't care."

Tracie let her head fall back as she let out an exasperated-sounding sigh. "He's getting away."

But Heath wasn't listening to her. He'd found the dent in her armor where the bullet had gone in. He plucked out the flattened bullet.

"Look familiar?" Tracie questioned.

He nodded. It looked much like the bullets that had hit him, only slightly less mushroomed. Of course, it had traveled a much greater distance before hitting her. He felt an overwhelming sense of gratitude that she'd worn the vest he'd given her only the day before. Something like a prayer of thanks rose in his heart.

"You need medical attention," Heath cautioned her as she sat up.

"Why? You didn't." She stood and grabbed her ribs where the shot had hit her, wincing visibly.

"You need medical attention," he repeated.

She bit her lip but straightened to her full height. "You got hit with six of these?" she whispered, pain in her eyes.

"Yeah. Kinda knock the air out of you, don't they?"

"Kinda," she retorted, rolling her eyes.

He grinned. With an attitude like that, he knew she would be okay. He pulled her into his arms, not caring who was watching.

But apparently she cared. "Heath, it's okay. Just a stray bullet. I'll be fine."

He stepped back and looked into her face. "You think that was a *stray* bullet?"

She looked down, not meeting his eyes.

"I've read all the files on our man Trevor," he continued, "and everything says he was an expert marksman. He fired three shots today, as far as I can tell. Two of them took out Sal. Are you going to tell me he didn't hit his intended target the third time?"

Tracie looked up at him, biting her lower lip.

"He waited until I stepped clear. He knew my vest blocked you the last time. Obviously he didn't want that to happen again." Emotion caught in his voice and he leaned closer to her. "Tracie, he's trying to kill you. *You,* understand?"

Pain filled her features as she finally met his eyes. "But why? Why me?"

Heath pulled her back into his arms. "I don't know." He'd been asking the same question himself. "But we need to find out."

Tracie still felt tightness in her chest as she prepared to head home at the end of the day. Whether the sensation stemmed from fear or her injury, she wasn't sure. Trevor had escaped once again. This time, she wasn't the only one to get a good look at him, though. Gary, John and Mack had returned with bewildered expressions on their faces, and had shakily admitted to chasing after a man they'd been sure was dead. It had opened up a whole new element in the case. If Trevor was indeed still alive, as now seemed likely, he was wanted on murder charges—for killing a man named Mitchell Adams six weeks before, and now, for killing Captain Sal.

When everyone else was gone from the office, Heath stuck his head around the side of Tracie's cubicle. "You done for the day?"

"Just finishing up," she said, filing copies of her last two reports. As she shoved the file drawer shut, pain speared through her blunt force trauma wound, and she held her hand to the spot, sucking in a sharp breath and struggling not to show how badly she was hurt.

But Heath was immediately at her side, his right hand covering hers as she pressed against the point of pain. "Are you sure you're okay? Maybe you should have X-rays."

"What are they going to do? Put me in a full-body cast?" She shot back.

Heath grinned at her. "You're amazing, you know that? I'm so lucky to have you in my life."

He reached out and smoothed back a few hairs that had come loose from her chignon.

Tracie froze. It would be so natural to lean into his arms, to let him hold her until she almost believed he could truly keep all the dangers that threatened her at bay. But she'd had a wake-up call the evening before when she'd discovered he had no relationship with God. She wouldn't allow herself to fall for him under those circumstances, no matter how drawn to him she truly felt. After the way he'd responded earlier that day when she'd been shot, she'd realized he'd begun to have feelings for her. She couldn't let that continue—for his sake, and for hers.

"Heath," she began hesitantly, looking up into his steel-blue eyes. "I need to apologize to you."

"For what?"

"I've been letting you get close to me, even though I barely know you. That's not normal for me. I don't move that fast."

An injured look flashed across his features.

Tracie wasn't sure how she could continue. She cared for him so much already. But she knew that getting involved with a man who didn't share her faith would only lead to more hurt in the future. "I'd like you to back off."

"I respect that," he said quietly, dropping his arms and taking half a step back.

She let out the breath she hadn't realized she

was holding. "Thank you," she said, though a part of her wanted to take back the statement, to draw him close again. She hardened her heart against the impulse.

"So I guess that means you don't want to have supper with me tonight?"

The way he was being polite about it only made her feel that much worse. "Sorry."

EIGHT

"Ready to head out?"

Tracie nearly jumped when Heath popped his head inside her office Thursday morning. She'd been up to her forehead in paperwork, frantically trying to make some headway.

"Be right there. Just let me run to the locker room a second." She squeezed past him and headed down the hall, checking her watch as she went. Tim's funeral was scheduled to begin in twenty minutes.

The tiny women's locker room was empty, as usual. There were only a couple of women who worked at the Coast Guard building. Tracie pulled open her locker, her mind scrambling over the details of the paperwork she'd deserted and the emotional upheaval of the funeral. She looked at her keys dangling from the hook inside her locker, and stopped short.

Something wasn't right.

A creeping sensation tickled her neck as she squinted at her keys. Then she smelled it, so faintly she almost could have thought she'd imagined it. She could have shrugged it off, but she'd learned otherwise. Bolting for the door, she hurried to where Heath stood waiting for her.

"Can you come take a look at this?"

"In the women's locker room?" He started in a lightly teasing voice, but then looked at her face and quickly sobered. He must have seen the fear in her expression. "What is it?"

She led him to her locker. "Look."

"I see keys."

"These are my personal keys, to my house and my car." Her hand trembled as she reached for them. With one finger, she turned the picture fob on her keychain, expecting to see Gunnar's face grinning back at her.

Instead, Trevor's sneering face leered at her.

She screamed and flew back.

Heath grabbed the keys from her locker. "Why do you have a picture of Trevor on your keys?"

"I don't know!" She covered her face with her hands, as though by shielding her eyes she could hide from the reality of the threat she'd just discovered. "It's supposed to be a picture of Gunnar on that side. I always hang my keys so his picture faces out, so I see him when I shut the door, and when I open it up again." It was a silly little ritual, and she felt foolish admitting to it, but it had often brought her comfort, especially on days when everything else in her life was cold and oppressive.

"So you think someone broke into your locker and changed the picture on your keychain?"

She fought to hold back her fear as she nodded.

"Who?"

"Trevor."

Heath raised an eyebrow at her.

"I smelled his cologne when I opened my locker. I noticed the keychain wasn't facing the right way, I smelled his cologne, and I called for you. And now you're here." She blinked at him a few times, trying to think of what else she was supposed to say, so overwrought with fear she could hardly think straight. She wanted to scream.

"What are these keys for?"

She pointed to each one in turn. "My house, my garage, my car, this building, my office, my file cabinet, the drawer of my desk."

"None of them are missing?"

"No."

"You're sure these are the original keys?"

"They look like them."

"How long has it been since you left them in here?"

"I came in at six. It's going on ten now."

"And we should get to the funeral." He settled a

hand on her shoulder, and she could feel the security of his strength as it settled her rattled nerves. "Is there any place in town that makes copies of keys?"

"Sure—the hardware store, the lumber company, probably the auto shop, maybe even some of the boating outfits, I don't know. How much does a key-copying machine cost? He could have gone anywhere, to Ashland even, or he could have his own machine. Do you want to ask around and see if anybody saw him?"

Heath looked down at her, his voice soothing. "We need to get to Tim's funeral. Don't worry about it right now. I'm with you. You're safe."

The smile she mustered up felt weak, but just being close to Heath made her feel safer. She tried not to consider what it might mean if Trevor had copies of her keys.

Heath was impressed at how quickly Tracie was able to pull herself together. Though she'd been horribly rattled by Trevor's terror tactic, by the time they reached the church, her features didn't look any more distraught than the typical mourner's. But once the service started, her eyes began to leak tears. Heath wished there was more he could do to comfort her, but since she'd asked him the day before to back off, he felt at a loss.

Ultimately, he knew the only way she'd be able

to move on was for them to catch Trevor and bring him to justice. Much as he wanted to focus on the minister's words, he couldn't seem to tear his mind away from what Trevor had done that morning. He could have easily taken the keys without anyone knowing it. So why had he gone out of his way to let them know what he'd done? Was it just to scare Tracie? From what Heath knew of Trevor, he just might be twisted enough to do so. But after the attempt on her life the day before, he suspected Trevor had more sinister intentions.

There was no burial service after the funeral. Tracie had informed him the frozen ground would be too difficult to dig through until spring thaw. Instead, the mourners gathered in the fellowship hall for coffee, bars and punch. As Heath stood beside Tracie, steaming foam cup in hand, he considered how quickly life could change. Just five days before, they'd stood there talking to Tim. Now he lay in a casket.

"Tracie, I'm so glad to see you!" An attractive-looking woman approached with a man on her arm. After a quick hug, Tracie introduced them as Abby Caldwell and Scott Frasier. Heath recalled their names from the reports he'd read and Tracie's discussion of their role in the case. Abby had been engaged to Trevor years before, though she was now engaged to Scott. She and Scott had discovered Trevor's body off the rocky shore of Devil's

Island moments before Tracie had arrived on the scene. The testimony they gave had fully corroborated what Tracie had told him.

"You made it." Tracie beamed at the couple through tear-reddened eyes.

"We had to." Abby drew Scott into their circle. "I should have been a better friend to Tim. I let him down."

"You were there for him when he needed it most," Tracie noted. "If he'd died two months ago, his story would have had a very different ending."

Heath considered Tracie's words as Abby agreed with her. He knew Tim had only returned to his faith in recent weeks—the minister had built much of his message around that fact. Heath wondered what kind of ending his own story would have if something were to happen to him. He wasn't entirely certain, and that thought made him feel uncomfortable.

"I feel so bad for Kathy Price," Abby's words pulled Heath's thoughts back to the conversation. "To have lost both her sons within a couple of months of each other. I can't imagine what she must be feeling."

Heath imagined Kathy would feel even worse if she knew one of her sons had killed the other. Realizing Abby had almost become a member of the Price family years before, he wondered if she'd have insights into Tim and Trevor's relationship no one else might have.

"What about their father?" Heath asked, wondering why she hadn't mentioned him.

Shaking her head, Abby explained, "Tom Price died in the Gulf War."

"Really?" Tracie raised her eyebrows. "I had no idea. Trevor never talked to me about his family."

"He used to boast about his father from time to time, years ago," Abby continued. "Apparently he was some kind of war hero."

"How did he die?" Heath prompted.

"The details are a little sketchy." Abby scrunched her face up as though trying to remember. "He was on a submarine that was lost during a mission. To my knowledge it was never found."

Tracie let out a small cry and quickly began to cough. Though he, too, felt alarmed by the revelation, Heath schooled his features into an expression of mild concern. "Are you okay?" he asked Tracie.

She held one hand to her throat and shook her head.

"I'll grab you some water," Scott offered and darted off, returning moments later and offering her the drink.

"Thanks," she sputtered after a slow sip. Then she shook her head and looked at Abby. "Sorry about that. Do you know the name of the submarine he was on, or any of the other men who were lost with him?"

"No," Abby shook her head. "I don't believe Trevor ever mentioned it. Why? Is it important?"

While Tracie took another sip of water, Heath decided the best way to find out if Scott and Abby knew anything else would be to let them in on their suspicions. After all, they'd been held prisoner in the sea cave by the diamond smugglers. They might have noticed some detail that could help the investigation. "We've retrieved evidence of submarine activity in the Devil's Island sea cave. There's a slight possibility it may have been a Navy sub that went MIA."

Abby gasped. "In the sea cave?"

"Yes."

Abby's eyes widened. "I saw it."

"You did?" Tracie asked incredulously.

"But Tracie and I were with you the whole time," Scott cautioned his fiancée. "How could you have seen it when neither of us did?"

"I remember looking around the cave, trying to take it all in so I could describe the place if I ever escaped. There was a large open space beside the boats, and I remember thinking it was strange, with so much space, that the boats would be parked so close together. And then I looked down into the water and saw—" her eyes widened "—this shadow."

"Could you describe it?" Heath pressed.

"It was a dark shape lurking under the water. It didn't just look like empty space, but like something was down there. It frightened me. But then, the whole experience frightened me so much I forgot all about it until just now when you mentioned the possibility of a submarine. Neither of you saw anything?"

"I recall the boats being close together as you said," Scott affirmed.

"I remember that much," Tracie acknowledged, "as well as the open expanse of water. But my attention was focused on trying to think how we might disarm our captors. I didn't pay any attention anything below the surface of the water."

"You know," Scott spoke up in a musing voice, "that would explain the trajectory of the bullets. Hadn't we determined that Trevor had been shot by someone standing on a craft at sea? But we never saw a boat."

"You're right," Abby snapped her fingers. "A submarine could have hidden much more easily. Even if it was still out there below the surface, it wouldn't have been obvious to us, since we were so distracted by the body."

"Good point," Tracie agreed slowly. "That's

just one more argument in favor of the submarine theory."

Scott shook his head. "That might explain what happened to Trevor's body, which is what always bothered me." He looked at each one of them in turn. "Didn't you guys find it strange that his body disappeared without a trace, even though we never saw any boats coming or going? If the guys who shot him had a submarine, they could have transported his body without our seeing them."

Tracie looked at Heath, questions and fears swimming in the tears that brimmed her eyes. Heath cleared his throat. "Actually, there may be more to your theory than that," he revealed, leaning a little closer. "We believe Trevor may still be alive."

With a gasp, Abby buried her face in Scott's shoulder.

"You know," Scott confessed, "I didn't want to say anything, but I always wondered if that was somehow possible."

Abby peeked out from behind Scott's arm. "We were actually just discussing the idea the other night," she admitted, straightening to face them. "But what makes you think he's still around?"

"Someone shot Captain Sal yesterday. A few of the guys got a decent look at the gunman and said he looked like Trevor."

"Wow," Abby's eyes widened.

"And that's not all," Tracie added. "My keys were tampered with. The picture of my dog was removed from my keychain and replaced with a picture of Trevor."

"You're kidding!" Abby gasped.

"I wish I was." Tracie listed off which keys had been compromised.

Abby shook her head in a sympathetic gesture. "How awful! So nothing of yours is secure. If my lease hadn't ended, I'd let you stay at my place, but I've been staying with Scott's mother while we get ready for our wedding."

"Thank you for the offer, but I'm sure I'll be fine."

"Do you think so?" Scott looked concerned. "Trevor's not someone you want to mess around with."

While Tracie dismissed her friends' concerns, Heath made up his mind to press her further on the issue later. He didn't want her all alone where Trevor could get at her, either. Still, he had some time before she'd be heading home. More urgently, he wanted to call back his friend from the Navy and find out if he'd had time to learn the names of the men who'd been on the *Requiem* when it disappeared. What had once seemed like an off coincidence now looked more and more like an actual possibility. Tom Price and his crewmates might have stolen a submarine from the U.S. Navy.

* * *

Heath wanted to wait until everyone was gone from Tracie's office before venturing in to tell her what he'd learned from his Navy friend. Finally, John and Mack packed up and left their cubicles, and Heath brought the list of names with him. But before he showed to it Tracie, he wanted to discuss something else that had been bothering him.

"Ready to head out?" he asked as he stepped into her cubicle.

"More than ready," she sighed, leaning back in her chair and closing her eyes for a moment. "It's been a long day."

"It's been a long week," Heath agreed. "A lot of things have happened, and I'm starting to feel a little suspicious."

"Of what?"

Heath sat in the chair across the desk from Tracie and leaned forward, speaking in a low voice. "Did Trevor know when we'd be coming to visit Tim? Did he time his brother's killing so we'd be the ones to find his body?"

While Tracie considered that question, Heath posed another. "How did Trevor know when he'd be able to sneak in and access your keys without being seen?"

Tracie leaned forward in her chair and faced him, adding, "How did Trevor know exactly when Sal was being transferred, hmm? Jake changed the time repeatedly. Only those people directly involved with the transfer knew what time it would take place."

Heath leaned forward across the desk, closer to her, glad she'd picked up on what he was hinting at. "How did Trevor know when we were going to be at his house? We'd only decided to visit the day before."

Tracie leaned forward a few inches more and whispered in his ear. "Do you think the office is bugged?"

"Could be," he whispered back, his lips skirting her earlobe. "But he'd have to have the whole place wired—your office, Jake's, mine, not to mention the truck. We haven't held any of these discussions in the same place. And if he had that many bugs going at the same time, he'd have to have that many people listening in. It doesn't seem feasible, but I'm still looking into it."

Tracie tipped her head back slightly. "Then what?" she asked, her voice soft.

Heath continued to whisper in a hushed voice, "a mole." He watched her carefully to see how she would respond to his suggestion. Though Jonas believed Tracie was the mole, Heath desperately hoped to learn it was someone else. Either way, he wasn't going to give up until he'd flushed out the leak.

To Heath's relief, Tracie startled at his words,

and pulled away far enough to look at him incredulously, "You mean a spy on the inside—one of us, reporting back to Trevor?"

"What else could it be?"

"I suppose it makes sense, but *who?*" She seemed genuinely disturbed by the idea, which reinforced his hope that she wasn't involved. "I don't know of anyone who felt any allegiance toward Trevor, and certainly if they had, the way he's been shooting at people would have to make them rethink it."

"He could have something over their heads. He could be threatening them. Who knows? People will do almost anything if they're desperate enough." Heath figured the only way Tracie could possibly be working for Trevor would be if she was being blackmailed—and considering how much she obviously feared Trevor, Heath couldn't rule out that possibility.

"But to work for Trevor." She looked as though the idea repulsed her. "I can't imagine." Then she leaned back in her chair and looked at Heath helplessly. "But then I suppose a number of things have happened lately that I never would have imagined."

"That's not the only thing I wanted to talk to you about," Heath continued.

Her eyes looked tired when she looked up at him, and he could see the dark circles beneath that showed how much the stress she'd endured was beginning to take its toll. "What else is there?"

"I don't want you to go home tonight."

Tracie blinked across the desk at Heath. The same thought had already occurred to her, though she didn't like it. "Because Trevor has a key to my house now?"

"Yes."

"Want to know what I think?" She'd gone over the issue in her mind a thousand times that afternoon already, and had reached a few conclusions. "I think if Trevor just wanted access to me, he could have made copies of my keys without ever letting on to me that he'd done so. No, I believe he replaced Gunnar's picture with his own to send me a message. He may not have even copied my keys." She planted her elbows on her desk and rested her chin in her hands.

"I think that last assessment sounds a little optimistic." Heath leaned forward until his own elbows rested just beyond hers. "What's the message you think he was trying to send?"

"He wants to frighten me. It's a scare tactic, that's all."

"He took a shot at you yesterday, and as far as we know, he had no idea you were wearing steel-plated body armor. He tried to kill you. The picture on your keys was a warning."

Tracie sighed and bit her lower lip. She didn't want to believe Heath. Though she'd almost convinced herself she truly believed Trevor wouldn't try to get to her inside her own home, Heath's words of caution rang true.

He looked at her levelly, his face close, his steel-blue eyes unswerving. "Isn't there anyone you can stay with? You still have family in the area, don't you?"

Tracie cringed. Sure, her mother and stepfather still lived in Bayfield, but she wasn't about to stay with them—not unless she wanted to endure their ongoing predictions that she would surely fail in her job, or quit, or possibly become the laughing-stock of the Coast Guard, if her stepdad really got going. "Not anyone I want to stay with," she told Heath firmly.

"And I suppose staying with someone from work—" he began.

"Nope. Most of the guys are single, so it wouldn't be appropriate for me to stay with them. Gary, John and Jim all have families, but they're living in cramped enough quarters as it is—they don't need an extra houseguest for an indefinite period of time. Besides, if Trevor wanted to sneak up on me, he wouldn't have left his calling card behind. He's just out to spook me. If I let him chase me from my home, he wins."

"If he kills you he wins," Heath amended.

Tracie persisted. "I have Gunnar. Trevor knows better than to try anything with Gunnar around—Gunnar would tear him to pieces, and he can smell him coming, too."

"Tracie," Heath leaned back in his chair and glowered at her, "Gunnar can't stop Trevor, and if you expect him to, then you're putting your dog at risk. Remember what you said when Tim died? That we should have forced him into protective custody, even though he refused it? I think you need to stay with your family."

She felt her mouth fall open as she realized what he was suggesting. "You wouldn't dare. You can't force me—"

"I don't want to," he interrupted her. "But I refuse to let you make yourself a target. I promised you I'd keep you safe. And I don't believe you'd be safe staying in your own home."

Pinching her eyes shut, Tracie considered Heath's words. She didn't want to stay with her mother and stepfather, but it didn't appear as though she had any choice in the matter. Trevor had taken away her freedom, along with her keys. "At least let me go home and get my things."

"No problem." His tone softened considerably and he smiled, his flashing dimple almost enough to make her forget he'd just won their argument. "Although I'd like to take you out to dinner first."

"Heath—" the fluttering inside her heart at his invitation set off warning bells inside her "—I asked you to back away, remember?" Her protest came out as a soft squeak, without her usual determination behind it. If she was honest with herself, she really wanted to have dinner with him.

"You need to eat a decent meal for once." He stood as though preparing to leave. "And besides, there's more we need to talk about."

Her curiosity immediately roused, she raised a questioning eyebrow.

"I got in touch with an old friend of mine from the Navy SEALs. He works with the Navy Records Department now," Heath explained.

Tracie jumped from her chair. "What? What did he tell you?"

"Names," Heath sighed. "I'll tell you over dinner, okay?"

Distracted as she was by the news he dangled in front of her, it didn't escape her notice that Heath had managed to get his own way. Again. "Fine."

"So what are the names?" Tracie asked Heath without preamble as soon as the waitress stepped away with their orders. It had taken all her willpower not to try to wrangle the information from him on the drive to the restaurant.

"These are the names of the four men who were on the *Requiem* when she disappeared." Heath unfolded a small piece of paper and set it on the placemat in front of her.

Tracie eagerly read:

M. Anderson

J. Kuhlman

T. Price .

J. Vaughn

"T. Price?" Tracie gasped quietly. "Tom Price died on the *Requiem?*" She looked up at Heath and her eyes narrowed. "Or was on it when it went missing?"

"Looks like it," Heath affirmed. "Trevor would have only been, what, ten years old then?"

"And Tim wouldn't even have been in school yet." She sat back in her chair and looked up at him. "What do you think? Is the *Requiem* our sub?"

Heath shrugged. "Do these names match up with the names of the men your father rescued on the day of his death?"

"No." Tracie had memorized the names of the four men years before, always alert for any mention of them, though she'd never run across any. She stared at the paper in front of her. "No, wait. If T. Price is Tom Price—" She bit her lip and looked at the other initials. "There was a Tom who was rescued from the sub the day my dad died—Tom London. And an M—Mark Smith. And the other two men both had first names that started with the letter J." She looked at Heath. "All four first initials match. Only the last names are different."

"Makes sense. Tom Price couldn't be Tom Price anymore, since Tom Price was supposed to be dead." He nodded slowly. "And it would make sense for them to only change their last names, since most people would call them by their first names, and they wouldn't want to give away their identities by accidentally answering to the wrong name. If they knew the Navy Records Division kept track of last names with first initials, then they wouldn't feel the need to change their first names."

"So Tom Price changed his name to Tom London and moved to Canada. Mark Anderson became Mark Smith and did the same."

"Not a terribly creative fellow, was he?" Heath kidded.

Tracie almost cracked a smile.

"What about our two J's?" Heath pressed.

"Morse and Blaine now," Tracie informed him in hushed tones as the waitress approached them with their salads. "One's missing, one's dead." She finished just before the waitress came within earshot, and surreptitiously slid the paper off the table into her pocket.

As the woman set their salads in front of them, Tracie reached for her fork.

Heath snagged her hand. "Want to pray?"

She looked at him for a moment as though he'd become a stranger all over again. "You want me to pray?" she asked, more than a little confused.

"Or I can."

"S-sure." She cautiously bowed her head.

Heath squeezed her hand as he prayed, "Almighty Father, we thank You for this food you've given to sustain us, and we thank You for always watching over us and keeping us safe. I pray You'd continue to protect us, and guide us to the truth about Trevor, and the *Requiem*, and Malcolm Crandall. Amen."

"Amen," Tracie echoed in a small voice. It took her a moment before she dared to raise her head. Heath had prayed. More surprising still, Heath had prayed they'd learn the truth about what had happened to her father. She hadn't even realized he knew her father's name.

She looked up at him, her heart swelling. It would be so easy to let herself fall in love with him. And if he really had a relationship with God, she'd have no reason not to. Hope filled her. "You pray now?"

"I've been trying," he admitted after swallowing a bite of salad. "I'm still working the kinks out, but I want to get to know God a lot better. Just like I want to get to know you better."

Tracie's mouth fell open. She didn't feel like she was in any position to make a decision about how she felt toward Heath—not with all the tumultuous events that had shaken her of late. Though she felt strongly attracted to him, under the circumstances she didn't trust her own judgment. Was she just looking for someone to lean on? Or was Heath really the man God intended for her? She couldn't begin to sort it out.

Heath's eyes didn't leave her face. "As friends?" he asked finally.

She gave a slight shrug. "As friends," she repeated, and turned her attention back to her salad, wondering if her life would ever become less complicated.

Tracie drove home with Heath's truck behind her, her heart doing a nervous dance every time she looked back in her rearview mirror and saw him following her. After dinner he'd driven her back to the Coast Guard station to get her car, and insisted on following her out to her place while she grabbed what she'd need to spend a few days with her folks. She guessed he still didn't quite trust her to go through with staying with her mother, especially since she hadn't called her yet to make arrangements for her stay. Heath was pretty smart that way.

Pulling into her driveway, she hopped out of her truck, mounted the front steps and paused.

Usually Gunnar came bounding through his

doggie door by the time she made it to the porch. Perhaps the sound of an extra vehicle had thrown him off. Shrugging off her concern, Tracie put her key in the lock and began to turn the knob. Then she heard a whimpering noise echo from the back of the house.

Gunnar. He sounded like he was in pain. No, more than that. He sounded like he was warning her.

Tracie froze with the doorknob half-turned. She could have bolted through the door and run to the kitchen to see why Gunnar was whimpering, but something told her that would be the wrong choice. She took a deep breath, trying to think. Then she realized something didn't smell quite right. Faintly, an odor like lighter fluid tickled her nostrils. And fainter yet, but still utterly unmistakable, the scent of Trevor's cologne.

Jerking the keys from the lock, Tracie spun around and leapt down the porch stairs. She hit the ground running as a loud explosion rocked the house behind her and the force of the blast threw her face-first into the snow.

NINE

Heath leapt from his truck and bounded toward Tracie. To his relief, he saw her raise her head even before he reached her. Pulling her up into his arms, he immediately began to assess the extent of her injuries.

"Are you okay? Are you hit?" He looked her over, brushing away the snow that clung to her hair and face.

She gripped his coat and stared up at him with desperate eyes. "Gunnar," she half shouted, half sobbed. "Gunnar's in there! In the kitchen—I heard him. He sounded like he was hurt." As she spoke, she pushed away his hands and flung herself through the deep snow toward the back of the house.

Heath realized she had every intention of going back in for her dog. His heart felt crushed as he recalled how much Tracie loved her dog. But having seen the blast, he knew Gunnar's prognosis couldn't be good. Still, the charge had been concentrated on the front of the house. The rear, where the kitchen was located, did not yet appear to be burning. Gunnar might still have a slim chance.

"Call for help," Heath shoved his phone into her hands and pushed her back toward his truck. "That's the best thing you can do for him right now."

"No." Tracie fought to push past him. "He's in there, I heard him. He's hurt." She pleaded with him with her eyes. "I can't just leave him in there to die."

Heath pulled her keys from her fear-stiffened hands. "I'll get him." He held up the key she'd pointed out to him earlier as being the key to her house. "Does this work on the back door?"

"Yes." Hope rose on her features. "Yes, oh, hurry. Hurry!"

"You stay here. Call for help. Promise me you'll stay?"

She nodded. "I promise. Hurry!"

He pushed her back toward the truck again and set off on foot, his mind ringing with every warning he'd ever heard, reminding him of the foolishness of going into a burning building without the proper equipment.

Heath found the back door and quickly got it unlocked. The smoke that poured out when he opened the door was concentrated in the upper part of the doorway—a good sign that the kitchen wasn't completely filled with smoke yet. Heath ducked his head and drew in a lungful of good air. In the SEALs, he'd learned to swim underwater for extended periods without coming up for air. He hoped the skill would be enough to help him out now.

Staying low, he rushed into the kitchen, quickly locating Gunnar chained to the legs of the kitchen table. The dog looked up at him with mournful eyes.

With the smoke alarm bleating diligently above him, Heath threw back the table and freed Gunnar's legs. Then he scooped up the heavy animal with a grunt and felt his air supply running out. He spun around to the back door and froze.

The fire had spread across the window curtains and wooden cupboards to the back of the kitchen, completely blocking the door. He was trapped.

Dear God, Heath thought, *get me out of here.*

Tracie clutched Heath's phone in her hands and watched for him to return. She'd relayed all the information to the dispatcher on duty. Now there was nothing to do but wait.

A minute passed. Two minutes. Where were Gunnar and Heath? Tracie thought about running inside after them, but she recalled the promise she'd made to Heath. If she went inside just as he was coming out another way, they might miss each other and both end up dead. She knew the facts, but it took all her self-control to keep her feet from flying across the yard to the back door.

As the distant sirens began to wail, Tracie realized something else. She'd made the wrong decision when she'd sent Heath inside her burning house to fetch her dog. Much as she loved Gunnar, she couldn't bear the thought that she might have sentenced Heath to die for the animal's sake. She held his phone tight as she crept cautiously toward the back door and prayed.

The back screen door flew open. Flames leapt high for a moment, and Tracie wondered how anyone could possibly be alive in there. A split second later Heath came leaping out, landing in the snow with a grunt and rolling, rolling.

Tracie rushed to his side. Her hand flew to her mouth as she realized he'd saved Gunnar.

"You've got him! You saved him! Are you okay?"

Heath stood slowly, still holding the dog. His reddened eyes stood out in stark contrast to his face, which was blackened from the smoke. He shook his head and trudged through the snow toward their vehicles at the front of the house, carrying Gunnar.

Tracie scrambled through the deep snow after him. They reached the front of the house just as

the emergency vehicles came to a halt, and firemen and paramedics leapt out, equipment flying.
Heath set the dog down on the open back end of
the ambulance.

"Oxygen," he gasped to one worker, who immediately shoved a mask over his mouth.

Tracie stood a few feet away, choking back a
sob as she watched Heath direct the paramedic to
administer oxygen to the dog as well. Gunnar's tail
gave a weak flop. Heath's shoulders heaved as he
drew in deep breaths of the life-giving air.

Approaching them both cautiously, Tracie slid
one hand up Heath's arm. "Are you going to be
okay?" she asked, her eyes filled with tears.

He drew a couple more deep breaths before he
moved the mouthpiece just enough to speak. "I
don't know. Depends on what the doctor says,"
he spoke quietly before clamping the mouthpiece
back down and drawing another deep breath.

A paramedic pulled her attention away. "Are
you all right, Miss?"

"Yes. I'm fine," she nodded.

"Is there anyone else in the house?"

Tracie shook her head. "No."

"We're going to head in. We'll drop your dog
off at the vet clinic, but we need to hurry."

She nodded and stepped back as Heath allowed
another medic to help him into the back of the

ambulance. Then they slammed the doors shut and drove away.

As she watched the truck disappear down the road, a lump rose in her throat. She knew Heath well enough to know he wouldn't have bothered going to the hospital unless he truly believed he needed treatment, which meant he had to have come close to death inside her house. And he could still die. Tracie knew smoke inhalation could be fatal even if the victim was conscious at the time of rescue, since the burning chemicals of the smoke would continue to work their destruction deep inside the lungs, their toxic effects multiplying even as the body tried to heal itself.

The realization hit her hard. Tracie could have killed Heath by sending him in there—by insisting on going home in the first place. The feeling that clenched at her heart was far more than guilt. She felt grief, a heavy sense of loss that filled her when she considered how badly Heath might be injured. In contrast, staying at her mother's place didn't seem so bad. She sighed. She had a phone call to make.

A screaming sound coming from the side of the road caught her attention. Tracie recognized her mother fighting her way past a couple of well-intentioned firemen. Tracie ran toward her. "Mom? I'm okay."

"Oh, Tracie," her mother pulled her into her arms.

"Benny heard it on the scanner and called me. What happened? Are you sure you're okay?"

"Yes, Mom, I'm fine. But I need a place to stay."

As she'd feared, her mother and stepfather started in immediately when she arrived at their house. "You just can't do this job, sweetheart. It's too dangerous," Marla Cooper whined before Tracie was even in the front door.

"Are you *trying* to get yourself killed?" Joe Cooper's question followed.

"Don't tell me this fire wasn't related to that diamond-smuggling business you all have gotten mixed up in. I heard what those investigators said."

"There's rumors down at the coffee shop, too. Tim Price was murdered. Whoever did it is after you, too, aren't they?"

Tracie kept her mouth shut, enduring their questions while she waited for the can of chicken noodle soup her mother had offered her to heat in the microwave. It had taken the firefighters a long time to put the blaze out, and the dinner she'd shared with Heath seemed like it had been days ago instead of hours. Once she had a little food in her stomach, she was going off to her room, which her mother had mostly converted into a sewing room since she'd moved away, but which still held her bed and a few of her things, and was still her room in her mind.

"It is those diamond-smugglers, isn't it? They killed both the Price brothers, didn't they?" Her stepdad leaned down to look into her face.

"It's under investigation. I can't tell you anything," she murmured, pulling her soup from the microwave and taking a sip. It was a little too hot, but rather than sit through any more nagging, she drank down a large gulp and checked her phone.

She couldn't stand not knowing how Heath was doing. At least the vet had called her after the ambulance had dropped Gunnar off, so she knew her dog was in good hands, though his condition was still touch and go.

Tracie still had Heath's phone since he'd given it to her before rushing into her house. The operator at the hospital didn't know anything, and only sounded annoyed when she pressed her for answers.

Gulping down the rest of the soup, Tracie held up her hand to their unrelenting questions. "I'm tired. Do you mind if I just go to bed?"

"Don't you want a shower? Something more to eat? Look at you, you're skin and bones. That soup isn't enough to keep a bird alive." Her mother dogged her feet all the way down the hall.

"I'll shower in the morning," Tracie said, closing the door before her mother could follow her into the room. She felt a little guilty as she hooked the simple lock that would keep her folks out, but she needed her sleep.

The dresser drawers still held some of her old clothes, and she pulled out a hopelessly outdated pair of pajamas, sliding into them and not even laughing when she saw her reflection in the mirror. After darting down the hall just long enough to brush her teeth, she locked her door again and slid under the covers, which still smelled of her mother's favorite fabric softener and somehow, of her childhood.

Tears streamed down her cheeks onto her pillow. Her parents' questions wouldn't have bothered her so much if she didn't believe them to be valid. Was she going to end up dead? Worse yet, had she led Trevor to her parents' house by coming here? And would Heath recover?

"Lord, please be with Heath. *Please*." She prayed over and over until she fell asleep.

Heath called Jonas Goodman from the hospital the next morning as soon as the doctor had cleared him of any lasting internal damage. His lungs might not feel the greatest for the next few days, and he'd have to watch for signs of pneumonia, but other than that, he was just supposed to rest. Easier said than done.

"Jake told me what happened," Jonas explained

when Heath began to update him on the previous day's events. "What I don't understand is what you were doing inside the house."

"Tracie's dog was inside there."

"The government has spent half a million dollars on you, and you're ready to throw it all away for a *dog?*" Jonas had never sounded so angry at Heath before. "Do I need to pull you off this case? Because I'm starting to have some *serious* reservations about keeping you in there."

"I have Tracie's trust," Heath informed his supervisor. "Even more so after rescuing her dog."

"Good," Jonas calmed down slightly. "And what does this trust reveal to us?"

"I don't believe she's on the inside."

"Why not?"

"This is the third time Trevor's attempted to kill her. He wouldn't try to kill his inside informant."

"Heath," Jonas's voice resonated with anger. "Have you been paying attention to this case at all? That's Trevor's M.O. That's how these guys work. They pop off their inside guys before they can squeal. The fact that Trevor is trying to kill Tracie only makes her that much more of a suspect. Wake up!"

Heath pinched his eyes shut against his boss's screams.

"Are you listening to me?"

"Yes."

"Then get on that girl and find out what she knows. She must know something, or Trevor wouldn't be working so hard to get rid of her. And whatever it is, we need to find out first. Do you read me?"

"Loud and clear."

"Good. You have twenty-four hours."

"Sir?"

"Twenty-four hours," Jonas repeated. "If you haven't learned her secrets by then, I'm pulling you off the case."

Heath placed the hospital phone back on its receiver. Twenty-four hours. It wasn't much time. He had to find Tracie—fast.

"You've got my phone and my truck." Heath's weary voice sounded so welcome to Tracie when she answered the phone at her parents' house.

"Are you okay?" she nearly screeched in relief.

"I'm invincible, remember?"

Tracie ignored his overly optimistic assessment. "How did you know where to reach me?" Her mother didn't even share her last name since she'd remarried, so Heath shouldn't have known to look up the phone book listing for Joe and Marla Cooper.

"Jake ratted you out."

She'd heard that line before, too. "I'm coming to get you."

Tracie borrowed her stepfather's truck for the drive to the hospital in Ashland. She'd never really cared for the odd formula that determined which scattered days she had off from work, but today she was relieved that her Sabbath fell on a Friday. Not only did she need the break from the craziness at work, but she figured it would take her most of the morning to get Heath, move his truck so she could get her car out of her driveway, and return her stepfather's truck to him. And that was even before she started thinking about checking on Gunnar or picking through the ruins of her house.

When she stepped into his hospital room and saw him sitting on the edge of the bed, looking a little deflated in yesterday's rumpled, smoke-stained clothes, she didn't think, but threw herself into his arms. She pressed her lips to his forehead before she came to her senses and held herself back.

"Are you really okay?"

"I've had worse." His voice sounded weak, but his blue eyes were still bright when they met hers.

She pulled him close again and stroked his hair. "I should never have asked you to go inside.

I could have lost you. You mean more to me than Gunnar."

Heath pulled his head back and looked at her quizzically.

When she realized what she'd said, she almost took the words back. But the more she thought about it, the more she realized it was true, not just because Heath was a person and Gunnar a dog, or because Heath had saved her life, but because of the depth of the feelings she had for him.

He pulled her close again and nuzzled her shoulder. "You mean more to me than Gunnar, too."

Tracie shook her head at his statement. Though she was pretty sure he'd only said it to be goofy, it didn't escape her notice that he'd gone into a burning building to save Gunnar. Apparently he'd be willing to do that much and more for her. She tried not to think too hard on the implications of that. "Let's get you out of here."

Checking out took longer than she would have liked, but with Heath's protective arm around her, she found she didn't mind so much. Then they hopped into her stepdad's truck and she steered them back in the direction of Bayfield.

"Something happened last night, Tracie," Heath began once they were on the highway.

"Lots of things," Tracie acknowledged. "For a minute there, I thought you were a goner."

"I thought so too. By the time I got Gunnar free from the table, the fire had spread all around me."

"Free from the table?" Tracie repeated.

"Yeah." Heath's voice still sounded sore. "He was chained to the table legs. He'd apparently been there long enough to drag the table part of the way across the floor."

Tracie gasped. "Do you think—" she started, fear filling her words.

"I think Trevor targeted Gunnar on purpose. You said he didn't like the dog, anyway, and if he knew how much you cared for Gunnar, he'd go after him just to rattle you." He coughed.

At the hoarse, raspy sound, Tracie cautioned him, "Don't strain your voice."

"Nah. Best thing for it. I have to work out all the junk that got in there."

Tracie wasn't sure how much she believed him, but she'd already learned he was the strong, stubborn type. She didn't figure she'd change him, and didn't really want to.

Heath continued. "I picked up the dog and looked behind me, and there was a wall of fire everywhere, right across the doorway. The room was full of smoke, and your smoke alarm wouldn't stop blaring."

Tracie had to smile at that last detail. "It's had lots of practice whenever I cook." Then she sobered. "So what did you do? How did you get out?"

"I prayed."

"Really?" Tracie's heart lurched.

"Yes. And God answered my prayer. He really did."

"I'm so glad." Tracie whispered. Heath had really started to develop a relationship with God. Her prayers were being answered, too. She blinked back the tears that blurred her vision. "So, do you think you'll keep on praying?"

Heath let out a long, slow breath and leaned back in the seat. "I tried again this morning. It still feels a little awkward. I thanked God for getting me out of there, for giving you the sense to get off the porch when you did." He paused. "I'm still fighting these doubts." His sore voice came out as a low rumble. "Would I have died in there if I hadn't thought to pray to God?"

"I don't know." Tracie kept her eyes focused on the road. "I thought more about what you asked me the other day."

"About why we bother to pray, even though God already knows what we need?"

"Yeah. I was thinking about what happens when I pray. It's not just about me asking God for what I want, it's about me asking God what He wants for me. Sometimes, God gives me exactly what I ask for, like last night when you asked for help getting out of the fire. But just as often, and maybe even more often, God shows me what He wants for me. He opens my heart up to something I hadn't even thought about." She stole a glance at Heath, who stared out the passenger window at the shore of Lake Superior, where waves crashed against the rocks below the highway.

She continued, "When Trevor first transferred to Bayfield and requested to work with me, at first I prayed God would send him away. But He didn't. Trevor stayed. I kept on praying, and after a while I realized God was using Trevor's presence to make me stronger. That's how I came to lead the self-defense class, which I enjoy more than anything. And I never would have started doing it if God had taken Trevor away the first time I prayed."

Heath turned and watched Tracie as she spoke. Her eyes were focused on the road, so he had the opportunity to take a long, hard look without her realizing how closely he was watching her. Her blond hair was swept back in a loose braid that fell down the length of her back. As usual, her face was free of makeup, her classic features beautiful without it. But far more than her outer beauty, Heath saw her determination and her faith. Her faith kept her strong. He wanted a faith like that.

He also wished he could tell Tracie who he really was. It wasn't only because he felt horrible about continuing to investigate her even though he felt certain she wasn't on Trevor's side. More than that, he wanted to share himself with her—every part of himself: past, present and future. But maybe there were things he could tell her without giving away his true identity. He said a silent prayer God would give him an opportunity to do so.

Tracie continued talking. "We have to learn to trust what God is doing is best for us, even when we don't understand it at the time."

"So you think Trevor's presence in your life is part of God's plan?"

She bit her lip and stared at the road. "Trevor is evil. He killed his own brother, he's been tormenting and trying to kill me. I don't believe that's part of God's plan at all. But the Bible says God makes all things work for *good* for those who love Him. Trevor's trying to ruin my life, but God took Trevor's evil plan and made it work for good."

"How?"

"He brought you into my life."

Heath watched Tracie blush and felt the same color rising to his own cheeks. "I don't know if I can make up for all the havoc Trevor has wreaked in your life."

She glanced at him, then quickly returned her eyes to the road.

He reached out and placed one hand gently on her shoulder. "But I'd like to try." Then he cleared his throat and felt the traumatized tissue stinging from the effort. "I thought we were supposed to take it slow?"

"Yeah." Tracie's blush deepened. "I'm not throwing myself at you, or anything, but I realized last night when you went in the house after my dog." Her voice faded.

He squeezed her shoulder gently.

"I realized how much you mean to me. I'm sorry I asked you to go in there."

"It's okay." Heath heard the rasp in his voice. "God worked it out for good."

TEN

Tracie slowed the truck to a stop at the side of the road near the blackened pile that only the day before had been her house. Heath was full of surprises. Though she'd thought him to be without faith, he was quickly opening up to let God into his life. She turned off the engine, pulled out the keys and looked up at him.

His hand still rested on her shoulder. As she leaned toward him his fingers laced back through her hair. "Can I kiss you?" he asked.

"I'd like that."

For a moment, all her worries about Trevor and Gunnar and her house and career all seemed to slip away, swallowed up by the comfort Heath offered her. Kissing him felt so right. She felt at home with him, even though her home was a pile of charred ruins. She didn't want the feeling to end, didn't want to return to the harsh reality she lived in. All too soon he pulled back.

"Taking it slow," he said, brushing her lower lip with his thumb as though tucking in the kisses he'd left there.

"Right." She took a moment to clear her thoughts. She was so glad God had brought someone into her life whom she could trust, after all she'd endured with Trevor. The thought of Trevor brought her back to reality and the business at hand. "Well, I talked to the head of the investigation team before I left to get you. They found the remains of a bomb at the epicenter of the fire, but the rest of the house is so damaged—" Her voice caught. Everything she owned was in ashes.

Heath pulled her against his shoulder.

"It's okay," she sniffed and straightened. "I'm fine. Just takes a little getting used to."

"We're going to catch him," Heath said, meeting her eyes with a determined expression.

"I hope so," Tracie continued, taking a shaky breath. "Anyway, there wasn't much left, and they didn't figure they'd find anything else, so they said I could come back today to see if there was anything I could salvage, or if I spotted anything out of place." She looked out the truck window to the blackened heap, unable to imagine finding anything recognizable among the ashes.

Heath squeezed her hand. "I'm here with you."

Hope leapt inside her. "You mean you'll help me?"

"You didn't think I was going to leave you here alone, did you? The house doesn't look all that stable."

Tracie sniffed and managed a smile. She didn't figure she looked all that stable, either, but thankfully he didn't mention that. "Thank you." She stared down the charred remains. "Okay, let's do this."

They slid out of the truck and trudged through the snow to what was left of the house. As the investigator had told her, not much remained. When Tracie thought about all the long hours she'd spent trying to fix the old place up and all the care she'd invested in making her home-improvements just right, her tears started running again. The immense heat of the fire had incinerated everything—wood, glass, even the nails. The metal legs of her kitchen stool rose above the ruins, though there was little left of the refrigerator that had once stood beside it. The shell of her stainless-steel kitchen sink rested on the floor

"How did they ever find the bomb?" Tracie mused aloud. What remained was so far removed from what she remembered, it was almost as though it hadn't been hers at all.

"When bombs explode, they project a blast outward," Heath explained. "The area immediately surrounding the bomb was probably the least damaged of everything, because it burned before the fire had gained its full strength."

"Makes sense," Tracie admitted. She crouched to inspect a pile of rubble on her back porch where her tool bench had once been. Holding up a charred hunk of metal, she told Heath, "My hammer, or what's left of it. It's a Gerlach."

"I know. I can tell by the curvature of the claw."

Tracie cocked her head to the side, thinking. "Heath Gerlach," she mused out loud.

Heath watched as Tracie made the connection between the brand name and his family's business. He'd prayed for a chance to tell her more about himself. Though this went beyond what he'd intended to confess, he recalled something in the Bible about God giving far more abundantly than he asked or imagined. So God had a sense of humor, too.

Since she looked as though she was about to drop it anyway, he reached out and took the hammer from her, weighing it in his hands. "Let's see, it's not from the pink series. That probably wouldn't have survived the fire." The company's least expensive line of tools was frequently given as high school graduation gifts, or to teenage girls when they got their first car. Though perfectly serviceable, they weren't very sturdy. "Red series?" he asked, naming the next level of tools, popular with handy housewives and adolescent boys.

Tracie looked at him with a slightly open mouth, as though she wasn't quite sure she recognized him. The abrupt revelation left him feeling a little off-kilter, too. "Nah, you wouldn't use the red line to renovate your house." He took a step closer to her. "Silver?"

"Yeah," she admitted softly. "I had the whole line."

"Hmm." He handed the charred hammer back to her. "Too bad you didn't buy the gold series. They have a lifetime warranty, no questions asked."

"It didn't seem practical at the time." Her voice still sounded distant, and she looked at him as though he was a stranger.

If her response to his family background shook her that much, Heath hated to think how she'd take the news that he was an undercover FBI agent investigating her for her role in the very diamond smuggling ring she'd helped crack. He kept his voice light.

"I've always said the silver series is the best value for your money. They're the same product as the gold series, except for the color and the warranty."

Tracie seemed to collect her thoughts. "So that's the family business, Gerlach Tools?"

"Yeah." He made a chagrined face.

"I was picturing something more along the lines of a shoe store."

"It's a little bigger than that."

"I guess so. You're one of the top names in tools, probably *the* top name."

"And one of the biggest employers in Green Bay County," he admitted.

"No wonder your parents were so busy."

"They were still building the company at that time. They considered their employees and customers to be their highest priorities." Heath explained. "It took a lot out of them. Now that they're more established, they have more time on their hands." He realized he was babbling and making excuses for them.

"Too late for you." Tracie looked at him with understanding.

Gratitude rose within him. She wasn't angry with him for not telling her? "Too late to do me much good," he echoed. "But they were good providers. Always gave me everything I needed—more than I needed, really," Heath didn't want Tracie to think his parents had been bad people.

Tracie's eyes narrowed in a thoughtful expression. "Do you think that's why—" she began, then stopped herself.

"What?" He pulled her closer against the chill of the air.

"Oh, I don't know. You said the other day you never understood why we need to ask God for things—that He already has everything and wants to give it to us."

Heath felt the corner of his mouth twitch into a smile. "And my parents always gave me *things* instead of time." The idea resonated inside him.

"Maybe that's another reason why we have to ask God for what we want," Tracie suggested, her voice thoughtful, and so soft the breeze nearly carried her words away. Heath leaned close to her as she continued. "Coming to God for our needs gives us a chance to be in relationship with Him. If we didn't need Him, we might never come to Him at all."

Heath dipped his head in a nod of affirmation, resting his forehead gently against her hairline, the hoods of their parkas forming a private nook for their faces. "I always wanted that relationship with my folks—not just the stuff they gave me, or nannies who doled out goodies to keep me quiet."

"Maybe it's not too late," Tracie whispered, her wide blue eyes staring into his.

"Maybe not," Heath conceded, though he harbored unspoken doubts. He felt grateful Tracie had taken the time to get to know him well enough to see into that hidden part of his heart. "I'm sorry I didn't tell you sooner. I try to live as though I'm not the heir of Gerlach Tools, and that doesn't always mesh with who people think I should be."

"Who are you, Heath?" Tracie asked, her expression open, heartfelt.

He wanted to tell her. He wanted so much to tell her. But it wasn't his secret to tell. Men died when secrets like his got spilled. "I don't know." Suddenly the injuries to his throat and lungs seemed to catch up with him. "Anything more you want to do here?" He looked around the ash heap. Nothing much remained.

"Not really." She held tight to the hammer, which, though charred, was still usable. "I need to get my stepdad's truck back to him and take my car into town, and then I'd like to visit Gunnar. I'm guessing you need your rest."

"I've got a mole to flush out," Heath reminded her.

Tracie looked disappointed. "You need your rest," she repeated, her voice firm.

"I'll rest when we catch Trevor."

She followed him to the truck in silence.

"I'm sorry I didn't tell you my family history sooner," he repeated when he noticed how sullen she remained. "If I'd have known how special you would be to me—"

"It's not about that," she said and sighed. "Heath, I wish you'd take care of yourself."

"I will," he promised, tilting her chin up with

his fingertips. He leaned close. "But I'm going to take care of you first, and that means catching whoever is after you." He left a single soft kiss on her lips. Then he watched her climb into the truck and drive off before he plodded back to his own truck. He had work to do.

Tracie put up with her mother's nagging for the entire drive back out for her car.

"I lost my husband to the Coast Guard. I don't want to lose my daughter, too."

"Mom, I'm being careful."

"Careful!" Marla Cooper pulled to a stop behind Tracie's car. She gestured to the remains of her daughter's house, deeply shadowed in the dim light of the setting sun. "You call this *careful?* Whoever's behind this is ruthless. I want you to get in a witness protection program, or a safe house, or something. You need out of this. You're going to get hurt."

"Mom." She looked at her mother patiently. "I just need to solve this, and then—" She didn't want to get her mother's hopes up.

"Then you'll quit?"

"I'm not a quitter," Tracie reminded her for what felt like the millionth time as she stepped out of Marla's four-wheel drive.

"I wish you would be," her mom called after her.

Tracie just nodded as she shut the door. She didn't figure quitting would do her any good at this point, anyway. And she had to catch Trevor, not just for Tim's sake, but for her own peace of mind. She wouldn't be safe until he was behind bars.

As the sound of her mother's vehicle faded down the road, Tracie crunched through the snow to her car. She picked through her keys, unfamiliar now that she'd removed the picture fob, and tainted ever since Trevor had touched them. She tried not to think about that as she slid into the cold seat and shut the door behind her.

A chill ran through her. She smelled him. Again.

"Put the key in the ignition and drive." Trevor's voice echoed through the vehicle as cold metal pressed against the base of her skull.

Heath couldn't shake the antsy feeling that something wasn't right. Whatever it was, he felt as though it was just beyond his reach; like a word on the tip of his tongue he still couldn't remember, it eluded him. There were so many things about this case that still didn't add up. He needed answers, but he didn't feel he could push Tracie any more, especially after what she'd already been through. Especially not when it concerned her father's death.

John, Mack, and Jim were all in the office when Heath returned.

Heath tried to keep his voice casual. "Can I ask you guys a few questions?"

"If you're wondering if things are always this exciting around here," Mack turned from his computer to face Heath, "they're not. This is usually one of the most boring posts in the Coast Guard."

"Hey, we're not boring," John defended.

"Not lately," Jim agreed, rising and tromping after the other guys as Heath led them down the hall to the conference room.

The men had been updated as the events involving Trevor's reappearance and the attacks on Tracie had unfolded, so Heath didn't need to fill them in. "I'm trying to sort out a motive here," he began, hoping to segue into Tracie's family history, but John interrupted him.

"Trevor's motive for attacking Tracie?" John clarified, then offered. "Trevor's had a thing for Tracie at least since high school. She was one of those girls who never seemed to realize guys thought she was beautiful. She was oblivious to Trevor's existence, and he hated that. When he came back to Bayfield, he immediately did everything he could to get close to her. Wouldn't take no for an answer. Still won't, obviously."

Heath looked at the other men to see if they had

anything to add. Both nodded, affirming John's words. Apparently they, too, had come to grips with the reality that Trevor hadn't died.

"But do you think that's everything? Tracie was telling me the other day that her father died in the line of duty fourteen years ago."

"Has it been that long already?" Jim ran a hand back through his thinning hair and gave a low whistle. "I must be getting old."

"So you worked here when Malcolm Crandall died?"

"Yeah."

"Do you know anything about how it happened?"

Jim looked back and forth between the two other, younger men. "You guys know any of this story?"

"I would have been in high school then," John offered.

"I'd just joined the Coast Guard, but I was stationed over in Duluth," Mack supplied.

"Okay," Jim sighed. "Well, it's all a little sketchy in my head. There was a submarine in the lake. Now, I've been around these parts all my life and never seen such a thing, but I hear some of those salvage ops run submersibles down. Whatever, that's their business." He paused. "What do you think this has to do with Trevor going after Tracie, anyway?"

Heath let out the breath he'd been holding. "I don't know. Too many things don't add up, and I figure any lead is worth pursuing." He let a look of challenge rise to his eyes as he looked each man in the face in turn. "Don't you think so?"

"Sure," Mack said, shifting in his seat. "Leave no stone unturned, and all that."

"Okay, well," Jim continued, "we got this call for help, a submarine run aground on the northern tip of the Devil's Island shoals—that's a shallow spot near Devil's Island. The men had air and all, but they couldn't leave the ship or they'd have drowned or died of hypothermia, whichever got them first. We're not really set up for that kind of gig, but Malcolm, he always loved a challenge, couldn't stand the thought of those men dying down there, so he said he'd make a dive and bring them up.

"Of course, by the time he got it all set up, the weather was going bad on him. He took a crew out. I was one of them. Most of us guys stayed on the boat, but Malcolm, he and Struck went down on a line. After bit, Struck comes up with these two men, said Malcolm was still down there helping the other two get suited up, should be right behind him. So we waited.

"The storm got worse. I don't like being out on the Gitchee Gumee in bad weather. Didn't like it then, like it even less now. After bit, up come these other two guys, saying Crandall's right behind them. So we stayed. And we waited. And when he never came up, Struck went back down.

"I thought we'd lost them both. I really did. Thought the rest of us might be goners, too, with that storm tossing us all over the place. But sure enough, Struck, he pulled Malcolm up out of the lake. He was dead by then, and there was nothing any of us could do to bring him back, but don't think we didn't try." Jim settled back in his chair, his story finished.

Heath was fairly certain he knew the answer to his next question, but he had to ask. "So the guy who brought up his body, Struck. That's…"

"Oh, sorry. Guess nobody uses his old nickname anymore. Jake Struckman. He was Malcolm's partner." Jim nodded. "Yeah, most people don't know this, but Malcolm Crandall would have been the Officer in Charge at Bayfield if he'd lived. Jake was next in line."

Trevor pushed the tip of the gun hard against the base of Tracie's skull. "Don't even think about trying anything."

Tracie could hardly think at all. Her heart pounded in her ears as she turned the key with trembling hands, put the car in reverse, and backed slowly down her driveway as Trevor had instructed. She could have kicked herself for not checking her car before she got in. It had never occurred to her that Trevor might be waiting for her in her car.

"We're going to take a little drive." Trevor's words barely registered. "Head for Red Cliff."

Tracie barely blinked, didn't respond, not even so much as a twitch of a nod, but she obediently pointed her car toward the Red Cliff Reservation. Her heart rose to her throat. He was going to kill her. She was sure of it. He might even get away with it, too. The unique laws that governed the reservation would no doubt hamper any investigation of her death—and that would be if anyone was able to guess he'd taken her to the reservation at all.

"Stay on the back roads." He jammed the tip of the gun harder against her head when she hesitated at the next corner.

Obediently turning in the direction he'd indicated, she frantically tried to think of a way out. She didn't dare attempt to make a run for it. Trevor was an expert marksman. He'd hit her before she made it out the door. And his position in the back seat left her no opportunity to try her self-defense skills, even if she'd have been able to summon the presence of mind to use them. No, her only shot would be to talk to him. One thought came to mind.

"Why did you kill your brother?"

"He was a little snitch, going to rat me out.

Besides, he was only my half brother. My mom cheated. He's the reason my dad went away to the war, and the reason he never came back. I didn't want a brother, and I never liked him. You, however," he stroked the back of her neck with the cold tip of his gun, "I always liked. A lot. It's funny. I always pictured the two of us getting along very well, kind of like you and your new partner." He pressed the gun hard against her soft flesh, emphasizing his words in a manner that would probably leave bruises—if she lived long enough for bruises to form there.

Tracie tried to stay on the offense. "So your father faked his own death and changed his name because your mother cheated?"

The angry push of the gun against her neck told her Trevor didn't like her asking questions. But he couldn't resist answering—if Tracie knew him as well as she thought she did, his pride was too strong for him to pass up an opportunity to boast. His favorite subject had always been himself.

"My dad got a better offer. He's a millionaire many times over *because* he faked his death. And he's taught me everything he knows. You can't prosecute a dead man. See, as long as everyone thinks I'm dead, I can change my name and live the life I've always wanted, with everything I've ever wanted. Including you."

"M-me?" Tracie couldn't keep the nervous

stammer from her voice. A bead of sweat ran down her forehead into her eyes. She blinked it away, convinced if she so much as removed one hand from the wheel, Trevor would end her life on the spot.

"Of course, you. The beautiful Tracie. At first I wanted to kill you. But when you wouldn't die, I thought of a better idea. I want what should have been mine all along. I want *you*. And I'm going to get you, too. Some friends of mine are throwing a little party tomorrow night. You're going to attend."

"Why should I?"

"Because if you don't, I'll kill you." He laughed. "See, I've got nothing to lose. I was going to kill you anyway. If you want to live, you have to do what I say. Besides, you can't resist, can you? It's the only way you'll get all the answers you've been looking for."

Tracie was pretty sure she knew most of the answers already. Trevor and his father were behind everything. "I don't need any more answers," she told him, wishing her voice would stop trembling.

Again, Trevor laughed. "Oh, you don't, do you? I thought you'd like to meet the man who killed your father."

For a moment, Tracie wasn't sure she could keep the car on the road. She fought to swallow back the anguished scream that rose in her throat. So her father had been murdered. She blinked back the thought and focused on her driving. They'd reached the edge of the reservation already. She schooled her voice into something remotely casual. She didn't want him to know how much his words had affected her. "Where are we headed?"

"The marina." The gun at her neck didn't waver. "That's where my ride is waiting for me."

It was getting a little late in the season to have a boat out on Lake Superior. The freezing temperatures they'd been experiencing had already begun to ice over some of the more sheltered portions of the lake's surface. Soon the icy patches would grow and spread into the lake, slowly overcoming the warmer mass of lake water, cooling and hardening it.

"Pull over," Trevor instructed her as her car neared the pier. "Park."

She followed his commands, her palms sweaty from fear.

"There's another question you haven't even thought to ask, and I'll give you the answer right now. Who is Heath Gerlach?"

"Heath?" Tracie echoed dumbly. She wanted to keep Trevor talking, but his revelations, on top of her fear, muddled her thinking.

"Of course, Heath," Trevor snapped. "Do you like him?" he asked in a menacing voice as he ran the tip of the gun up and down her neck. "You love him, don't you Tracie?" He chuckled. "If so, maybe I'll let you see him again. Maybe I'll let you watch me destroy him, *slowly and painfully.*"

Tracie clenched her hands around the steering wheel. She had to warn Heath. But first, she had to get away from Trevor. She prayed God would give her a way out.

Trevor chuckled to himself. "Heath Gerlach is not who you think he is. He works for the FBI. Ask him about it. He's investigating you for your role in the smuggling ring. That's why he wanted to get so close to you. It's not because he cares for you. He's just been using you so he could find out what you knew. But don't worry, we'll get even with him." Trevor leaned back and stretched. "I'm in the mood to kill someone."

Tracie braced herself for the end.

But instead of a bullet, she felt him press a paper into her hand, which was still clutched tightly to the steering wheel.

"Here's your invitation to the party. Dress pretty—it's a formal affair, and I want to have the most gorgeous date there." He opened the back door. "I'm going to leave you now. Don't try anything. My guys have their guns trained on you as we speak, and I'd hate for them to ruin your beautiful figure before the ball." He stood. "Good night, Tracie," he said in a hard voice just before he slammed the door shut.

Tracie watched through the windshield as Trevor strode toward the pier. In the fading sunlight, she could just make out the hulking, domed form of a submarine, its jagged mast piercing the night sky. Trevor walked out onto the craft and stepped down through the hatch, closing it after himself. Then the whole thing slowly sank in the water as it backed away from the pier into the depths of the great lake.

Tracie slumped her head against the steering wheel, her body trembling, her mind spinning. Her father had been murdered, and Trevor was buddies with whoever had done it. He wanted her to come to his party and meet the guy.

Worst of all, Heath had betrayed her. Her heart clenched at the thought. She'd trusted him. No, worse than that, she'd fallen in love with him. But it had all been a lie all along.

Something in her heart cried out, refusing to believe Heath had truly deceived her. Perhaps Trevor had made it up. She had to believe Heath over Trevor. Choking on her hope, she threw the car into gear and peeled out, sniffing back tears as she tried to level her thoughts. She'd find him. She'd ask him. He'd tell her Trevor had been lying. He *had* to.

She drove back to town, fighting back tears so

hard she could barely keep her grip on the steering wheel.

Just as she'd figured, Heath's truck sat in the Coast Guard lot. Tracie jumped out and hurried into the building, wiping back the tears from her face. She darted through the door, poked her head in Heath's cubicle, and then finally found him sitting with a few other guys in the conference room, talking.

They looked up and fell silent when she came through the door.

"Tracie?" Heath jumped up from his seat and hurried to her side. "What's wrong? What happened?"

She took a deep breath. She would be calm. She would *not* make a scene. "Who do you work for, Heath?"

Confusion warred in his features. "What do you mean?"

"Are you an FBI agent?" She put it to him bluntly. "Are you investigating me?"

He reached for her, the guilty look on his face telling her everything she needed to know. "I can explain."

She pulled her arm away. "That's okay. Trevor already did." Unable to stand there and look at him knowing he'd deceived her, she spun on her heels and hurried away.

Heath ran after her. "Tracie, please. This isn't

as bad as it looks." He reached for her as they left the building. "What did Trevor do to you? What did Trevor *say*?"

In the parking lot, she turned to face him, not caring how miserable she looked with tears running down her face, not bothering to wipe them away. "I don't know why I should care," she half shouted through her sobs, "but Trevor said he was going to destroy you. So maybe you should get out of here before he kills you, too."

Her words proved adequate to keep Heath off her heels. She ran for her car before he could come after her again, quickly cranking the engine and throwing the vehicle into gear. She had a lot of things to sort out, and she didn't have much time. According to the invitation Trevor had pressed into her hands, she had less than twenty-four hours before her date with death.

Heath fought back the urge to tear off after Tracie, throw himself at her feet, and beg for her forgiveness. No, much as he wanted to make her understand what he'd done, no amount of explaining could change the facts. He had lied to her. She had every reason to hate him.

Besides that, Trevor had made contact with her and threatened her. If he was going to protect her, he'd have to hurry.

He got on the phone with Jonas immediately.

"Your gig is up, Heath," Jonas said instead of "hello."

"What? It hasn't been twenty-four hours."

"I just talked to Jake. Your cover's been blown. Apparently Tracie announced your undercover status in front of everyone."

Heath cringed. How could he have kept Tracie from doing that, when all along he'd been prevented from letting her know who he really was?

The FBI officer continued. "There's nothing more you can do for us."

"No, Jonas, I need to—"

His supervisor cut him off. "You're a liability, Heath. One we can no longer afford. I expect to see you in my office promptly at eight tomorrow morning."

"Jonas, I—" But the phone at his ear had gone dead.

It was over.

ELEVEN

Joe Cooper handed the phone to Tracie the moment she stepped into the house. "Who is it?" she mouthed to her stepfather.

"She said she was from the FBI," Joe answered with a concerned look.

"Yes, Tracie Crandall?" The voice on the other end began as soon as Tracie said hello. "My name is Martina Morgan. I'm with the FBI. I understand Trevor Price has contacted you."

"Yes," Tracie answered, wondering for a moment how the woman knew. But then, she'd announced the fact loudly in a room full of people, including an undercover FBI agent. And it was their job to know things like this.

"We have a delicate operation already underway and need your assistance to complete the mission." The woman paused. "Your help may mean the difference between catching Trevor Price, and letting him go free."

Still feeling stunned, Tracie rushed to agree. "Of course. Whatever I can do to help." She wasn't sure yet what she was agreeing to, but it didn't matter. She'd do whatever it took to put Trevor away for good.

Heath went back to his apartment and threw his things into his duffel bag. He didn't know how he could help Tracie, and since Jonas had taken him off the case, he didn't know what else to do. If he wasn't in his office by 8:00 a.m. the next day, he'd no doubt lose his job. It was bad enough that his cover had been blown, though he didn't know how Trevor had figured out his identity. Apparently Tim had been right. They had no idea how deep the operation really went.

Falling down on his knees beside his bed, he buried his face in his folded hands and groaned, "No, God, please. I won't leave her. I can't let her face Trevor alone." Knowing how much she feared and hated Trevor, he couldn't leave her in the hands of the man who only wanted to torment her.

"Dear God, I need Your help. I've *got* to rescue Tracie. I've got to. I can't just walk away and leave her to Trevor. I can't stop loving her." A sob tore through his chest, sending the bruised muscles in his back into spasms of pain.

He waited, distantly aware of the grit on his carpet and the musty smell of dust bunnies under the bed. Remembering what Tracie had said about prayer, he tried to sort out what God was up to. Could God take all this evil that Trevor had intended and make good come out of it? Would God change the situation for him? Or was God simply using the situation to change his heart?

He rolled into a ball of pain on the floor and pinched his eyes shut against the horrible reality he'd found himself in. With a gasping breath, Heath laid his heart out. "Okay, God. Whatever You want. Whatever You want me to do, I'll do it. I'm through trying to do this my way. Please guide me."

Then slowly, like the rising of the sun in the morning, one moment a sliver of light peeking over the horizon, imperceptibly growing to a brilliant glowing orb, possibilities began to occur to him. Favors he could call in. Long-forgotten contacts he could reach out to. A plan began to form in his mind. Sketchy, yes. A long shot? Certainly.

But it was something.

Tracie stood in front of the mirror looking at the stranger reflected back at her. A shimmering silver dress sheathed her body, coming to a stop just above sparkling diamond-studded shoes with heels so high she could hardly walk in them. Matching chains of diamonds spun like gossamer threads down from the halter neck, across the open back, crisscrossing her bodice like a spider's web.

Diamond earrings dropped from her lobes, which were already starting to throb in protest; bracelets dangled from each wrist, and two enormous diamond rings adorned her right hand.

The only thing she recognized was the fear in her eyes.

Tracie closed her eyes, hardly able to muster a sigh. The heavy fake lashes on her lids were more than she wanted to heft open. She hadn't slept since Trevor had put the gun to her head. Too much had happened. Martina had called, she and her men had swooped in with a sleek tractor-trailer, its interior part lab, part communications center, part dressing room, and now they were hurtling down the long stretch of highway that led to the Canadian border and the address on the invitation Trevor had given her.

"Wake up!" Martina snapped her fingers in front of her face, and Tracie pulled her eyes open.

"These earrings are so heavy." She lifted them with her palms to ease the pain.

Martina batted her hands away. "How else do you expect to communicate with us?" Martina had already explained how the communication devices in the earrings worked. "Keep the earrings on, and whatever you do, don't lose your rings." Tracie held up her right hand, where GPS tracking devices were embedded in both of the diamond rings she wore. "If we lose you, we'll lose you, and you *don't* want to do this on your own."

"Right." Tracie heard her voice waver, and felt her head tremble when she nodded. She couldn't do this. There was no way she could pull off this look, not even for a second. Going to Trevor's party meant walking straight into the lion's den. She could barely walk at all in the high heels they had her wearing.

"Let's wear this one, too," Martina held up a small diamond hairclip. Tracie's blond hair fell in long, loose waves down her back. Martina stuck the clip by her temple.

"What's that one do?" Tracie asked, doubting it was there just to keep her hair out of her eyes.

"It's a recording transmitter. You won't be able to use it to communicate with us, but it will record everything you hear and transmit the recording to a file on our computer." Martina took a step back and looked her over. Apparently satisfied, she announced, "I'm going to check with the guys on our status. You stay here, and stay beautiful." The woman blew her a kiss as she left.

Tracie did not feel encouraged. Everything was falling apart around her. Heath had used her. He didn't love her, didn't even care about her. He was probably laughing right now about how naively she'd fallen into his trap. But instead of anger, all she felt was a heart-clenching sadness.

"I'm an idiot," she informed the stranger in the mirror. "After all the lies he told me, I still care for him." She sniffed and rummaged around in the knapsack she'd brought until her fingers found what she was looking for. Of all the things to bring with her to an FBI bust, she'd grabbed a Bible. But she needed strength and comfort now more than anything, so she spilled open the pages and scoured the red letters for whatever encouragement she could find.

She found Jesus on the Mount of Olives in the Gospel of Matthew. *My soul is overwhelmed with sorrow to the point of death.* Christ's words touched her heart, sparking recognition. She kept reading.

My Father, if it is possible, may this cup be taken from me. Her soul resonated with the words. She sat still, begging God to free her from the mission she didn't want to accept, but couldn't seem to escape. Jesus hadn't wanted to drink from the cup of death. He'd prayed for God to take it from him. But God hadn't taken it away. Jesus had gone to his death. Tracie thought about the questions Heath had asked her, about prayer and how it worked, or didn't work. Why hadn't God answered his only Son's prayer? It didn't make sense.

"Jesus had to die to save the whole world," she mused out loud. "I don't need to save anybody. I just want to go home." But her conscience protested her own words. Trevor had killed his own brother without remorse. He'd tried to brutally murder her and Gunnar and had threatened to go after Heath. No, she wasn't just in this to save her own skin. Trevor would stop at nothing. He'd keep on killing. He had to be stopped before he trampled on more innocent people in his quest for power and wealth. He had to be brought to justice. But how could she ever stop him?

Popping her eyes open, she continued reading from the open Bible on her lap. *My Father, if it is not possible for this cup to be taken away unless I drink it, may Your will be done.*

Four words jumped out at her with shocking clarity. *Unless I drink it.* Her breathing came fast and she dropped her mouth open as she stared at the Bible on her lap. Christ's cup *had* passed from him, *but only by his drinking of it.*

The realization hit her stronger than any jolt of caffeine. God *had* answered Jesus' prayer—the hard way. And the only way she was going to get through this was to face it head-on. Energized by the startling revelation, Tracie closed the Bible and stood, grabbing the earrings and hooking them back through her earlobes. Then she stared down the beauty in the mirror. "Let's drink this."

Heath looked up from checking coats in the coat closet, discreetly studying the elaborate ice-palace ballroom in the remote mansion near the Canadian border. Tom London's place was unlisted, but Heath had reached a friend in the FBI who'd gone out on a limb to send him the address just in time. He counted three officers he knew, looking stiff in their tuxedos. Hopefully there were more out there he just didn't recognize. Tracie was already woefully outnumbered.

Though he'd originally hoped to bring in a couple of his friends to help, it had taken all his finagling just to get in the door. Oddly enough, he felt at peace about that. God had brought him this far, and he felt a growing certainty that no number of extra men on his side would make any difference in the long run. If God intended for him to rescue Tracie, he'd make it happen, no matter how slim his chances seemed. So he checked in coats and waited, alert for any sign of Tracie.

Finally, at ten minutes to eight, he saw her enter with Oleg and Olaf, twin blonds each the size of a refrigerator. Heath had worked with them before. Oleg took the heavy fur from Tracie's shoulders, stepping toward the coat room. For the first time, Heath got a good look at her.

His throat tightened. She looked radiant—not just on the outside, dripping in diamonds—but her whole being sparkled. Her eyes lit up as she threw her head back and laughed at something Olaf said, and a burst of air blew in the open door, sending her long golden hair swaying around her shoulders.

Oleg handed over the fur, and Heath kept his chin down, his face half turned away. The blond boys weren't supposed to know he was there. The last thing he wanted to do was alert Tracie to his presence. She had her work cut out for her already without having to think about him.

He hung up the fur and turned back just in time to see her disappear through into the ballroom, practically floating in heels he couldn't imagine anyone walking in. Two coats later he slipped away, praying he blended in a little better than the stiffs he'd already spotted.

Tracie kept close to Oleg and Olaf as she circulated through the room, hoping to spot Trevor before he found her. He'd gotten the jump on her too many times recently. Waiters in white jackets circulated with exotic food and drinks held high on silver trays. She sampled a fat shrimp perched atop a mound of crushed ice. Like everything else around her, it sparkled.

Diamonds seemed to be the theme, and Tracie couldn't help wondering if all of the gems around her were the same as the fakes Trevor had been helping to smuggle. When she tried to count the gems their dazzling brightness only made her eyes water. There were too many, she decided, as she made her way toward the front of the room where an elaborate display of large diamonds atop black velvet was roped off from the crowd.

Though elegantly-dressed people packed the room, Tracie wasn't the only one who appeared not to know anyone else. Very little chatter rose over the soft music of the orchestra.

That fit. According to Martina's brief explanation, most of the people invited were innocent of any direct connection to Trevor. They appeared to have come from all over the world. They were investors, most of them, lured by an invitation to take part in a deal too appealing to pass up. Part of her role in being there was to help the FBI sort out the bad guys from their innocent victims.

Tracie didn't have long to wait for Trevor. As the band played a buoyant tune, a flat-panel screen dropped behind a podium at the end of the room nearest the diamond display, the lights dimmed, a spotlight shone and Trevor appeared, looking larger than life and deceptively handsome in his tuxedo. He approached the dais and welcomed everyone, first in English, then in French. As he spoke, translations of his words in several languages appeared on the screen behind him.

"Our previous creation, which we like to call the blue diamond, was successfully marketed for nearly twenty years before jumpy gemologists turned the market against it." Trevor's smooth

speech made it sound as though his team of diamond smugglers had been victims of an unfounded
boycott.

As Tracie understood it, there were a lot of
fine lines that had been crossed. Though chemically and physically identical to natural diamonds,
Trevor's gems were grown in a lab. There was
nothing illegal about them per se. Anyone could
own them and, considering how long they'd been
smuggled into the U.S., probably many people did.
No, the crime was in passing them off as natural
diamonds, whose value could be hundreds of times
higher than that of the synthetic gems. Essentially,
Trevor and his associates were guilty of cheating
and lying, as well as the other crimes they'd com-
mitted to hide their business, including smuggling
and murder.

Trevor continued his speech. "Though our gems
appear clear under natural lighting, their blue color
becomes immediately apparent in UV light, as
my lovely assistant, Tracie, will step forward and
demonstrate."

Tracie's eyes widened at the sound of her name.
She glanced to her right and her left, but Oleg and
Olaf were nowhere in sight. The spotlight found
her and she stepped forward under Trevor's cold
gaze.

Lord, I'm trusting You to see the way out of this,

because I don't, she prayed silently as she held her head high and moved forward.

Trevor motioned her into place beside him while the lights changed once more, and a glaring black light obliterated the crowd and even the features of Trevor's face. Gasps and murmurs echoed through the ballroom, and Tracie looked down.

Against the shadows of her darkened dress the diamonds cast a phosphorescent blue glow, their crisscrossing pattern appearing to ensnare her like a net, each brilliant gem uniform not only in size but in color as well. She knew from her research that such consistency was unheard of among naturally-occurring diamonds. Her dress had to be made with fakes, along with her shoes and the rest of her jewelry, including her earrings, whose broad baubles she could see glowing blue on the edges of her peripheral vision.

"Inspect them for yourselves," Trevor continued, reaching down and, before Tracie even realized what he was about to do, sliding the rings from her right hand and tossing them into the eager crowd. "You will find them to be of the highest quality." Deftly he removed her earrings. Tracie tried to snag them back, but they were in the hands of the partygoers almost as quickly as they'd left her ears.

She was on her own, with no way to communicate with Martina or anyone else who worked for the good guys. They wouldn't even be able to find her. Trevor had neatly taken care of that.

But how had he known? The FBI had dressed her, apparently using gems they'd confiscated as part of their investigation. Who had leaked the details of her ensemble to Trevor? Or had his people simply recognized their own product when she'd arrived? Had his removal of her microphones and tracking devices simply been a coincidence? Tracie recalled what Tim had said the day before he'd died. *You must not realize how deep this thing goes.* Who else was secretly on Trevor's side? Who was the mole Heath had been searching for?

While Tracie's mind spun with questions, Trevor boldly proceeded to announce that a new product line would be introduced later in the evening. Then the lights rose and his hand clamped possessively around her shoulder.

Tracie glanced around the room, frantically trying to locate Oleg and Olaf, and simultaneously praying she wouldn't reveal her fear to everyone. But no one looked familiar, and Trevor quickly encircled her waist with one thick hand.

"My lovely assistant," he growled, his eyes narrowing like those of a fox moving in for the kill. "I can't wait to see you in your next costume. But first, we have some catching up to do. Ah, here come your men now." Trevor tipped his head toward Oleg and Olaf, who swept forward, each cupping an elbow and sweeping her in the direction of a side door.

For one disoriented moment, Tracie thought they'd come to her rescue. But then they pushed through the door with Trevor at their heels and shuffled her into a waiting limousine. Trevor slid in the other side and the locks snapped down with a final click.

She was trapped.

Heath saw Oleg and Olaf sweep Tracie away, though he couldn't comprehend why they'd cooperate with the enemy. He'd already discovered one of the FBI men out cold in a closet—where the other two were, he didn't know, but they weren't anywhere around. He was on his own.

Fortunately he was near the front exit, and quickly slipped out. Vaulting off the veranda, Heath was just quick enough to catch sight of Tracie being shoved into a waiting limo. For a fleeting moment he caught a glimpse of her face, her eyes searching for some means of help or escape, her panic when she found none. He recalled his promise to be there for her, to protect her from Trevor. No doubt right now she thought he'd failed her.

The limousine rolled forward and Heath ducked low behind a snow-covered hedge, taking a moment to pop out the collapsible nylon snowshoes he'd stashed in his back pocket. He slipped the webs over his shoes, their sleek ski-like soles just enough to keep his feet from puncturing through the crust of deep snow. Once the limo was past, he darted across the snow-buried grounds along the well-lit path to the shadows. He'd have to move quickly, or he'd lose them.

His snowmobile was parked on the far side of the wall, or would be as long as no one had discovered it. A long expanse of snow-covered lawn stretched between the house and the six-foot-high enclosure. Heath ran as fast as his snowshoes would carry him. He leapt for the wall at a dead sprint, grabbing hold of the top ledge and pulling himself up, heavily favoring his uninjured arm. Swinging his legs over, he dropped to the ground on the other side, started the engine and took off in the direction of the front gate where he'd seen the limo headed.

With his headlight turned off to prevent detection, Heath sped forward, peeling off his snowshoes as he went. Even with all the wealthy guests in attendance, there wasn't a great deal of limousine traffic, and Heath spotted the vehicle easily. A quick glance at the plates confirmed it was the same car he'd seen the twins shove Tracie into.

Wishing he'd had more time to scope out the area, Heath kept his snowmobile in the ditch as he followed the limo down a winding road. The neighborhood was an enclave of mansions, a semi-gated community of the ridiculously rich. He supposed most, if not all of them, had earned their money off the diamond-smuggling business, whether directly or indirectly. Making the connections between the guilty individuals would be the tricky part, but that was the least of his concerns.

Heath had to catch up to Tracie. He cringed at the thought of her alone with Trevor in the limousine. Fortunately, they weren't in the car for long. The limo turned at the next driveway, which had neither a wall nor a gate, but was instead lined with poplars. Though they'd shed their leaves for the winter, their low, spread-fingered branches provided some measure of cover for him in the darkness.

The moment he heard the limousine stop behind the sprawling Swiss-styled chateau, Heath killed the motor on the snowmobile. Snapping his snowshoes back on, he crept forward in the shadows just in time to see the light of an open door framing armed men who handed Trevor an assault rifle before escorting Tracie into the mansion.

Heath watched the door shut after them. His heart sank. He couldn't just go barging in after Tracie. Something told him these guys were the type who'd shoot first and ask questions later. Looking around desperately for a way to get into the house, Heath noticed how the steeply-sloped roof nearly met the high-piled snow in places. It wasn't much, but it was better than nothing.

With movements as smooth and silent as he could make them, he wriggled his way onto a dark corner of the roof and shuffled upward. Thick snow and ice slowed his progress, but Heath managed to pull himself across the heavy snow up to a skylight, where he peeked in.

Kitchen. Nobody in sight. He swung himself up, braced his feet against the top edge of the skylight, and scooted along the roof to where another glassy bulge betrayed the builder's preference for natural lighting. Heath peeked down through the clear glass into a lavishly decorated bedroom suite.

Tracie.

She held her head high, though he could see her fear in the rapid rise and fall of her diamond-draped décolletage.

The big guys had their guns pointed at her, but other than that, she appeared to be unharmed. Heath wanted to throw himself down through the skylight, but with so many gunmen in the room, he'd be dead before he hit the floor. That wouldn't help her any. He sat quietly, watched and waited.

Below, Trevor pulled out a pair of handcuffs and linked one ring over Tracie's wrist before coupling it to his own. Only once she was securely cuffed to him did he send the gunmen out, though he kept an assault rifle slung over his shoulder.

Heath's heart beat so hard he could feel it in his throat. With every breath he prayed God would somehow get Tracie out of there, though he couldn't imagine what it would take. He felt completely helpless watching the events unfold below him, unable to do anything to stop them.

In spite of her circumstances, however, it appeared Tracie still had the presence of mind to do something. Though Heath couldn't see her face from his vantage point high above, her body language seemed to indicate she was talking to Trevor. She extended her free hand toward him and laid her palm against his suit jacket, then tossed her long, loose hair back.

Suddenly, in a move that caused him to startle and nearly lose his perch on the roof, Tracie swung her leg high, delivering a perfect round-kick to Trevor's temple. Her captor dropped with a thud Heath heard through the snow-packed roof. Tracie's ruse had worked. Trevor hadn't even seen the kick coming.

As Heath watched from above, Tracie sprang into action, patting down Trevor's pockets, pulling out a ring of keys and freeing herself from the handcuffs. Quickly she cuffed Trevor to a narrow spot on the carved bedpost, below where the ornate carving spread wider, effectively trapping him. Then she took his gun and slid the strap over her own shoulder before looking around. Heath saw her hesitate as she faced the door. There were probably armed men on the other side. No, her odds wouldn't be good if she went through there. She took a few tentative steps in the direction of the door.

Heath took advantage of her distance from the skylight and drove the heel of his shoe as hard as he could through the skylight. Though it proved to be tough tempered glass, it was no match for his pent-up fury, and it shattered, spilling glass shards onto Trevor's still body below.

"Tracie!" Heath called as she spun around and looked up.

A welcome grin broke out on her face as she recognized him. For a second, all he could do was grin foolishly back. Then he realized they might not have much time. Even if there was no alarm on the skylight, the men would likely have heard the crash of breaking glass. They could come rushing in at any moment.

"Hop up on the bed," Heath instructed in a hushed voice as he used the soles of his shoes to clear the glass shards from the sill, then leaned as much of his body as possible down through the gaping skylight.

Tracie stretched upward, her hands still a few feet below his. Glancing about, she grabbed a silken, bronze-colored throw that was draped across a bench by the fireplace, and tried tossing it up to him, but the lightweight material taunted them both by drifting lazily down before ever so much as tickling the tips of his fingers.

With a nervous glance to the still-unconscious Trevor, Tracie snatched up the ring of keys she'd used to unlock the handcuffs and quickly tied the key ring to the tassels on one end of the drape. This time, when she flung it upward, Heath grabbed it easily.

As soon as Tracie had a tight hold on the other end, he began to haul her up, his injured back crying out in protest. She was nearly level with the skylight when Trevor groaned and opened his eyes. Curses erupted from Trevor's mouth as he reached for Tracie and grabbed hold of her foot.

TWELVE

Heath flung himself backward down the roof. For a moment, he feared Tracie's tenuous gasp on the silky fabric would fail and she'd be pulled back down into the room below. But she held on tight and he pulled her free, half falling down the roof with her tumbling after him.

Trevor's angry shouts echoed up through the open skylight as Heath and Tracie scrambled through the deep snow toward where he'd left his snowmobile. He didn't have time to stop and put on his snowshoes, but he figured Tracie was far worse off in her open high heels. She flung the drape around her shoulders, the lightweight fabric offering her otherwise bare arms meager protection against the bitter cold.

"You drive," he shouted as they reached the snowmobile. She hopped into the seat and scooted forward, making room for him to jump on behind. He pulled the keys from his pocket and cranked the engine. She tore out just as the door opened behind them and armed men came spilling out.

"Where to?" she shouted over her shoulder.

"This way." He reached his arms around hers and steered them toward the road, trying to cover as much of her body as possible with his. Not only was she undoubtedly freezing, but he knew there was no way she was wearing adequate body armor under her dress. Once again, he'd have to shield her from whatever shots were fired.

"Want me to turn on the headlight?"

"Let's not make ourselves a target," he said straight into her ear as her loose hair spilled over him. "The moon is bright enough for us to see." He kept his arms around her and pointed them toward the distant marina.

Headlight or not, the guys in the SUVs behind them didn't seem to have any trouble keeping up. Tracie left the road and took off across country, making the most direct path toward the harbor, but it didn't stop their pursuers. They turned onto the drifting snow and followed them.

"Where am I headed?" Tracie asked as they neared the marina, bullets whizzing past them as they went.

"I don't know. The pier?"

"What's our getaway vehicle?"

"*This* is our getaway vehicle." He thumped his hand on the snowmobile's handlebar.

Tracie groaned but gunned it for the pier. In spite of the deep snow, the four-wheel-drive vehicles were still behind them, fishtailing like crazy but refusing to get stuck or fall behind. Heath felt a bullet strike the broad steel plate that shielded his back. "Keep your head down!" he instructed Tracie as he ducked as low as he dared.

He flinched as a bullet grazed the back of his leg. The SUVs were closing in behind them, but they drew closer to the pier, where a lone black speedboat sat in the thin film of ice at the end of the dock.

"Looks like something Trevor would drive," Tracie muttered as she headed for it. She pointed the nose of the snowmobile directly at the long pier. With the end of the dock racing toward them, Tracie slowed the snowmobile, braking hard as they slid toward where the dock dropped off into open water. For a second, Heath feared they'd overshot it, but the snowmobile screeched to a halt on the wooden planking just before the end. They dived into the boat.

There was nowhere else to go, and the four-wheel drives were nearly to the pier. Given enough time, he may have been able to hotwire the boat, but their pursuers were far too close. Heath grabbed the rifle Tracie had slung over her shoulder and wondered how many bad guys he could pick off before they took him out. It would depend on how drastically they were outnumbered.

"Stay down!" Heath shouted as Tracie rushed to the helm. He crouched low and turned to face their pursuers.

"I think I can start the boat," Tracie called back to him. "I still have Trevor's keys."

Or at least that's what he thought he heard. He'd started shooting, taking out the front tire of the lead vehicle as it closed in on them, causing it to skid sideways and block most of the road. Another SUV slammed into it while a third swerved wide, careening up on two wheels before slamming back down and continuing on.

Heath aimed at its tires.

Suddenly he heard an engine starting up behind him, and a split second later, their boat began to move. He took out a tire on the third SUV, then noticed the rope unfurling from their boat as they moved away from the pier.

"Wait a second, we're still tied up," he cautioned Tracie as the boat began to build its speed.

"I'm not waiting for anything. Take care of it," she snapped back.

Heath aimed the gun at the mooring and snapped the line with a single shot. "Got it."

The men jumped from their vehicles ran to the end of the pier. They raised their guns and took aim.

"Down!" Heath shouted, throwing himself toward Tracie. He covered her with his body while she held down the throttle with her hands, and he reached one arm up, keeping the steering wheel steady while bullets glanced off the rails above them. They didn't have to look where they were going. There was nothing but open water in front of them for the next thirty miles. The boat sped into the silent night.

"Stay down," Heath insisted as Tracie began to wriggle from his grasp.

"I think we're clear," she whispered.

He waited another moment until the sound of gunfire had faded away completely, aware of how ice-cold her bare arms felt under his fingers in the freezing night air. Finally he relaxed and poked his head up. There was nothing but fog and the silent sea around them. Even the shoreline had disappeared.

Tracie slowed the motor somewhat when she realized they were all alone in the middle of the vast, open sea. She slid herself up onto the captain's chair before she caught her breath and began to shiver, for the first time granting herself the luxury of wondering what Heath was doing rescuing her, anyway. He looked amazing in his tuxedo, which only made her feel more confused about how she was supposed to respond to him.

When Heath quickly peeled off his jacket and threw it over her shoulders, Tracie slid her arms through the sleeves, too cold to protest his gracious offer. The jacket held his familiar smell. She pulled it tight around her, telling herself she needed the warmth more than the comfort it brought her.

"How did you get the boat started?" he asked, his arms draped over her shoulders.

"I still had Trevor's keys." She shrugged, attempting to casually throw off his arms. She was still far too angry at his betrayal to allow him to get close to her again. She'd learned her lesson. "Can you take the wheel while I look for a blanket or something?" The slender windshield of the open boat offered little protection from the bitterly cold night air.

"Sure."

Though she noticed Heath hobbling slightly as he lowered himself into the seat, she told herself she didn't care what his condition was. After all, he'd lied to her and betrayed her. Anyway, at the moment, she cared a lot more about finding a way of keeping herself warm. She had plenty of questions to ask him, but her interrogation could wait until she stopped freezing so badly. She could barely feel her frozen feet as she stumbled toward the benches that lined the sides of the boat.

Moving the cushion out of the way, she lifted the seat and peeked into the storage space below, rummaging tentatively with her hands in the darkness. "Life jackets, life jackets," she muttered, pushing them aside. They wouldn't offer much warmth. Then she pulled out a box. "Hey, this is a Coast Guard first-aid kit. Trevor must have stolen it."

"I doubt there's any law he hasn't broken," Heath said.

She closed the lid and tried the benches on the other side. "At least he thought to steal some Coast Guard blankets, too." She pulled the blankets out. "These are the best you can get for warding off hypothermia." She wrapped one around her shoulders and carried the other two back to the captain's seat where Heath had one eye on the compass, keeping the boat pointed straight south in spite of the fog. He snapped on the headlights, but the thick fog only reflected the light back in a solid wall. He turned the headlights off again.

"I can take the wheel," she offered.

Heath rose slowly, grimacing as he attempted to straighten his right leg.

"What's wrong? Did you pull a muscle?"

"I'll be fine. They just nicked me." He accepted the blanket she offered him and pulled it over his shoulders.

The man was too stubbornly strong for his own good. Tracie felt concern for him rising in spite of the anger she held toward him. "With a bullet? Do you need first aid?" She turned back for the first aid kit she'd seen.

"I don't think it's too bad. Honestly."

His self-assessment meant nothing to Tracie, knowing what injuries he'd previously disregarded. She grabbed the first-aid kit and crouched down to inspect the damp spot halfway between his ankle and his knee. Heath clicked on a small light above the helm.

Tracie rolled up the cuff of his pants and was relieved to find the cut wasn't very deep, though it still wasn't pretty. "You've got to stop getting shot at," she chided him, searching through the first-aid kit for the right size bandage.

"Only if you do," he chided her back, then reached for the radio. "I'm going to try to call in the cavalry to pick up Trevor. I don't know how fast those guys will be able to change their tires in this snow, but they'll be sitting ducks for a couple more minutes, at least."

Tracie listened while Heath contacted his FBI pals and conveyed the information they'd need to nab Trevor and his cronies. He sounded frustrated as he attempted to sort out what had happened back at the gala.

"Oleg and Olaf appeared to be working for Trevor," he noted. "I don't know if somebody got their wires crossed or what." He ran an anxious hand down over his face while the person on the other end reported that two agents had been tied up in the basement, and another had awakened in the closet with no memory of how he'd gotten there.

"I don't know who's calling the shots on this one," Heath began, only to be cut off.

Tracie couldn't quite make out the response, but Heath's reaction was clear.

"He wasn't anywhere I could see. Goodman may be a maverick but he's not sloppy. Anyway, we did the hard work already. Just make sure they don't get away. Thanks." Heath sighed and set the radio back in place, shaking his head.

Tracie finished gently pressing a large bandage daubed with antibacterial ointment into place over the wound on Heath's leg. He reached for her.

She tried to shake her head at him, but she felt so stiff from the cold she could barely move. Her teeth began to chatter convulsively.

"Here, we've got to get you warm." He locked the steering wheel into position and stood, wrapping his arms around Tracie as she straightened.

Tracie wanted to fight him. The last thing she needed to do was snuggle into his arms—he'd already used that trick to wriggle his way into her heart before. But she hadn't known he was investigating her when she'd let him get close the first time. Now she knew better.

Still, she felt so cold, and as the terror of what she'd just experienced began to sink in, she shivered both inside and out. She promised herself she wouldn't allow her feelings for him to get the best of her as she leaned against the warmth of his solid frame. Summoning up some of the anger she felt toward him, she infused its snap into her voice. "What are you doing here, anyway?"

"I had to come after you."

"Why? Is that part of your investigation? Do you still think I might be in cahoots with Trevor?" She spat out the words, welcoming the fresh pain of his betrayal. She needed to remember why she couldn't trust him before she relaxed her guard and let him hurt her again.

"No. It wasn't my theory. You were part of the assignment, that's all. I never meant to hurt you— all I wanted was to learn the truth."

"By living a lie?"

"I did my job." Heath's shoulders tensed around her, as though he was wrestling with what to tell her. "Believe me, once I got to know you, I wished I could just be myself."

His words made it sound as though he'd been playing a role with her. Tracie wondered how much of the man she'd fallen in love with really existed, and how much was just an act. She had obviously never really known him. Her heart hurt even more than her feet, which were throbbing from the pain of the cold and their tribulation inside the impractical footwear they'd been forced into for so long.

She blinked into the night sky, for the first time realizing how thickly the fog blanketed their tiny boat.

"Are you sure being out here in the middle of the lake is a good idea?" she asked.

"We're going to be fine," Heath insisted. "God provided us with this boat, and you with the keys. He'll see us through." Heath met Tracie's eyes, facing her fear with certainty. "I know He will."

"Since when are you and God so close?" she asked, her voice almost a whisper.

"Since I almost lost you." He pulled his arms tighter around her, drawing her more snugly against him. "I made a mistake, Tracie. I never should have kept my true identity a secret from you. But if I hadn't been assigned to investigate you, we never would have met, so I can't regret my assignment too much. Can you forgive me?"

"Forgive you?" She peeked warily up from the warm shelter of the blanket. "I don't know how I can ever trust you again. I pushed aside my own personal policy to get close to you because I thought you were someone I could trust, and look how it turned out. You fulfilled my worst fears."

Heath didn't know how to respond to Tracie's rejection. Still, she was cold enough to let him hold her, and he savored the feel of her in his arms. He wished there was some way he could go back in time and change things, to do it all again a different way so she wouldn't have been deceived. It wasn't just the fact that he'd betrayed her—it was the result of that betrayal. She'd ended up fed to the lions, walking alone straight into Trevor's trap. His heart bled for her and the fear she must have felt.

"I'm so proud of you," he told her softly as he stared ahead into the fog.

"Why?" she sniffed.

"You took out Trevor. I watched you from the skylight. I wanted to dive down and rescue you, but I didn't have to. You rescued yourself. It was amazing to watch. He never saw it coming."

Tracie peeked up at him again, the corners of her eyes curling into the slightest of smiles. "I chained him to his bed, too. Just like he chained Gunnar to the table." Her expression sobered. "But then I didn't know how I was going to get out of there. There were so many armed men, I didn't know how I could possibly fight them alone."

Heath smoothed her hair back from her face. "It doesn't matter now. You're out. It's behind you." He looked up from her face just in time to see a faint beam of light blinking distantly off to their right through the thinning fog. He cut the boat's throttle.

Tracie sat straight up. "What is it?"

"Lighthouse," he said, pointing to the beacon as it slashed toward them through the night sky.

"I know where we are," Tracie said, blinking as the beam cut past them again. "That's the beam from Devil's Island. It's visible for fifteen miles in clear weather. We probably aren't that far away if we can see it through this fog."

Oddly enough, rather than hope, Heath felt a twinge of disappointment at the discovery. They were nearly home. Once their journey was over, he'd no longer have any excuse for spending time with Tracie. She'd said she couldn't trust him again. He couldn't blame her after his betrayal, though he wanted more than anything to continue his relationship with her. "Can you navigate back to Bayfield from here?"

She made a face. "Not in this fog. The islands are tricky enough when you can see them coming. Besides, the shallow waters and sheltered coves fill with ice earlier than the open lake. Who knows what we might run into?"

Heath pinched back a smile and unlocked the steering wheel. "What do you say we camp out at Devil's Island until the fog lifts?"

"Great idea. Maybe we can get in out of the cold." She slumped down into the seat beside him as he pointed the boat in the direction of the blinking beam.

"No problem," Heath said, putting the idling

boat back in gear. The idea of spending a little more time with Tracie appealed to him strongly, but something uneasy roiled in the pit of his stomach. He didn't like Devil's Island, especially not the sea cave. But Tracie had been frightened enough lately, so he didn't mention his fears to her as he steered the boat into the darkness.

Tracie didn't want to say anything to Heath, but she wasn't entirely comfortable with the thought of going back inside the cave at Devil's Island. She'd had only negative experiences there, but more than that, she felt a distinct uneasiness at the idea, a deeper chill than the cold of the winter air that pressed against them. But she shook off her worries, telling herself her fear stemmed from too much stress and lack of sleep. Surely the worst was behind her.

As he lined up the boat to enter the pitch-black darkness of the sea cave, Heath turned on the boat's bright headlights, which immediately illuminated the brownstone back wall of the outer cave.

"That's odd," Tracie reacted. "The hidden wall was open when we were out here on Tuesday. You didn't close it when we left, did you?"

"No. You were with me the whole time. We left it wide open." He idled the boat to a stop just inside the smaller outer cave. It bobbled slightly in the icy waves, nosing against the false back wall.

"I thought so, but I was so disoriented that day." She shook her head. "So someone has been out here. But who would be crazy enough to come out to Devil's Island in this weather?"

Heath looked at her solemnly. "Only someone who's really desperate, I'd guess." He stood and moved toward the side of the boat.

"What are you doing?" she asked.

"I'm going to open it. According to the report you insisted I read, the latch mechanism is over here somewhere, right?"

Tracie shuffled closer to him, careful to keep her blanket securely wrapped around her, protecting her from the cold. "Are you sure we want to do that?"

"It's less than thirty degrees out here," Heath noted, gesturing to the crystalline shards of ice forming on the water all around them. "But I'm willing to guess it's closer to forty or fifty degrees in there. That's still cold, but it's a lot warmer than out here." As he spoke, he stepped closer to her and placed one hand on her arm.

She shook off his hand. Though his words made sense, her sense of foreboding grew. "Heath, please, we don't know who closed the cave door, or why."

"Well, who could it have been? Probably someone from the Coast Guard, don't you think?"

"If they did, wouldn't we have heard about it?

Nobody had any reason to come out here." The only ones who knew about the cave were the members of the Coast Guard who'd been involved with the search for Marilyn Adams, and the smugglers themselves. Due to the ongoing investigation, the fact of the cave's existence hadn't been released to the general public. She bit her lip thoughtfully.

"Who else knows this cave is out here?" Heath asked. "The smugglers? Trevor should be in custody by now."

Tracie shook her head. "Trevor told me he was going to introduce me to my father's killer tonight, but he never got around to doing so. Unless your FBI guys got him, too, then my father's killer is still at large." Her words were cut off by a ratcheting boom as the secret door began to rise. Tracie blinked at Heath. "How did you do that?"

"I didn't do it," Heath began.

Tracie's eyes widened as the open expanse of cave was revealed by the rising wall. The boat's headlights pierced the darkness, reflecting back off the brownstone interior. Combined with the glow of the overhead lights inside the cave, it was enough for Tracie to see clearly the dark, hulking form that lurked in the water.

A submarine floated inside the cave, its rounded hull a dark greenish-brown, its conning tower rising above them, with a jagged mast that scratched the ceiling of the cave. The cave door settled open with a decided groan, followed by near silence and the gentle lapping of the waves.

"Then who—" she started to ask quietly.

"I did." A voice echoed up from the long pier that ran half the length of the cave.

They both turned, and Heath's body sagged as he let out a relieved-sounding breath. "Goodman! You captured the *Requiem?*"

"Of course." The voice echoed through the emptiness as a man stepped toward them. "You didn't think I'd let you take all the credit for breaking up the smuggling ring, did you?"

Heath hurried to the side of the boat, tugging Tracie after him. "It's okay. It's my boss from the FBI," he explained. Tracie quickly slipped her aching feet into the diamond-covered high heels before disembarking.

"So." The man spoke again as they hurried across the cold walkway toward him. "I didn't see you in my office this morning as planned," he said, staring Heath down. But then his scowl was replaced with a toothy grin and he chuckled. "Seems I'm not the only one who likes to do things his own way. Now, would you like to see inside? She's a beauty."

Tracie hesitated. Her father had died on that submarine. She wasn't sure she wanted to go anywhere near it.

Heath's boss must have sensed her hesitation.

"It's a lot warmer inside the sub than out here," he noted with a wink.

Though he made an excellent point, Tracie's heart still beat hard as she approached the submarine. Heath supported her as she stepped unsteadily onto the hull in her stiletto heels, and then down into the hatch. When she stepped off the ladder at the bottom, she turned and found herself in the brightly-lit control room. She blinked a few times against the suddenness of the light and shuffled out of the way as Heath stepped down beside her.

She was surprised to see three other large men besides the man who'd greeted them. He came down last, pulling the hatch closed tight behind him.

"Ready for the nickel tour?" The man nodded to them and led them through a brief passage to a cramped room with curtained bunks on one side. "Here we have the crew's quarters," he announced, nodding to one of the men who'd entered the narrow room behind them, who then closed the door.

The creeping feeling along the back of Tracie's neck became too much for her to ignore. It wasn't claustrophobia, although the coffin-like bunks along the wall didn't offer the room much in the way of breathing space. No, something wasn't right. Heath was the only man on the sub whom she knew, and even he had recently betrayed her.

As the shifting bodies in the tight space sent her shuffling closer than she'd have liked to Heath's boss from the FBI, she pasted on a smile and said, "I'm sorry. I don't believe we've been introduced. I'm Tracie Crandall."

"Pleased to meet you, Tracie." He extended his hand. "My name is Jonas Goodman."

"Jonas Goodman," she repeated, the name registering as too familiar to be merely a coincidence, as the man's other hand snapped forward and he clicked a cuff around her wrist. "You mean Jonas Vaughn, a.k.a. Jonas Blaine," Tracie corrected him. She tried to pull her arm away, but the cuff was already closed tightly around her slender wrist, and just as fast, Jonas jerked her arm toward a pipe that ran the length of the ceiling, clamping the other side of the handcuffs tight to the pipe.

"That's right," Jonas said, clearly unaffected by hearing his aliases revealed. Before she could recover from her shock, he pulled her other wrist up and cuffed it to the pipe as well.

Tracie glanced to Heath, half expecting to find he was in on Jonas Goodman-Vaughn-Blaine's plot. Instead, she saw Heath's bloodied head lolling from side to side as the two big guys who'd come in behind her cuffed his unconscious body to another pipe.

She whipped her head back toward Goodman, who'd retreated along with his men to the doorway behind them. "You killed my father!" she shouted after him as the other thugs headed down the passageway.

"I did," Jonas smiled, "and if you don't give me the answers I want, I'm going to kill you, too." He looked back over his shoulder in the direction the other men had retreated, then chuckled. "I'll be right back." He didn't even bother to shut the door behind him.

Heath fought back against the heavy darkness that shrouded his eyes. Through a throbbing headache he heard his father's words to him the last time he'd been home.

"I just don't understand what you think you've got to prove. Your mother and I love you. We want you to come home. That FBI work you do is dangerous. We don't want to lose you. *We don't want to lose you.*"

The last sentence taunted him, ricocheting around in his mind like the glancing shot of a bullet. Regret surged through him, because for the first time he could begin to envision a life for himself running the family business. If he had Jesus in his heart and Tracie at his side, he wouldn't be alone anymore, not even at Gerlach Tools.

Too bad the realization had come too late.

Heath fought back the nausea that rose in his throat as he pulled his head up from his concussed stupor and looked across the tiny crew's quarters to where Tracie stood. Both her hands were cuffed to the pipe on the ceiling, her Coast Guard blanket lay crumpled on the floor, and his tuxedo jacket dwarfed her slim figure as she shivered in her diamond-shrouded dress. He'd promised to protect her, but he'd unknowingly delivered her into the hands of her father's killers. She had every reason to hate him.

"Tracie, I'm sorry," he began in a whisper.

She ignored his apology. "Where are they going? What are they doing?"

Heath hadn't realized the men had left them alone, but he now felt the subtle, silent vibrations that meant the submarine was getting underway. "He's probably telling the other guys where to take us."

"And then what? He's just going to leave us for dead somewhere?"

Her assessment sounded so final, he didn't want to think about it, or give her any room to think about it. Ignoring her question, he clarified, "So J. Vaughn was Jonas Vaughn."

"Yes." Tracie shot a fiery look back at him. "Jonas Vaughn became Jonas Blaine, a.k.a. Jonas Goodman."

"And who was the other J?"

"Jeff Morse, a.k.a. Jeff Kuhlman. He died in Canada eight years ago. Ironically, he was the only

one of the four men who I was ever able to personally contact."

"Shortly before he died?" The bump on Heath's
head made it harder for him to follow what had
happened.

"Yes. I didn't know until you found the names of
the men who were lost with the *Requiem* that his
real name was Kuhlman. I didn't know anything
about him. I searched for years for the men who
were in the sub when my father died. I finally
found Jeff, but before I was able to meet with
him, he died when his truck went off the road in
a blizzard."

"Makes sense." Heath paused, wondering if
Jeff Kuhlman's accident had really been acciden-
tal. These guys seemed to knock off anyone who
threatened them. "I'm sorry. I never imagined, not
in a million years…" He let his words fade away
as the muffled sound of footsteps drew closer.
"Jonas," Heath said in an icy voice as the man
he'd trusted entered the tiny room.

"It's time," he announced, approaching Tracie
with a key in his hand. "You have a decision to
make, but before I tell you what your choices are,
you need to understand what a lucky girl you are.
Trevor Price likes you. He's rich. He's powerful.
He's handsome. And he wants you at his side."

Jonas trailed the key along Tracie's jawbone,
outlining the curve of her delicate features. "So

here's the deal—Tracie Crandall is going to die tonight, and it's up to you to decide whether that death is real or only a cover. If you choose to go to Trevor, we'll give you a new name, a new identity, and you can enjoy the best things money can buy. Or we can simply kill you now."

While Heath watched, furious at his own help-lessness, Tracie's eyes met his. Her voice was as cold as the ice on the lake. "Kill me now."

With a chuckle, Jonas noted, "Funny, that's the same choice your father made, right before I ripped off his oxygen supply. You see, he'd seen too much. And you've seen too much." Jonas looked from Heath to Tracie. "You two have made a lot of trouble for me today. I was headed to the party when Martina reported in and told me she'd picked up Trevor where you left him, handcuffed to the bed."

As he spoke, Jonas backhanded Heath in his wounded arm. Heath winced, but refused to give Jonas the satisfaction of hearing him cry out in pain. Jonas dropped his friendly tone. "How dare you override my direct orders?" he shouted. "Now I have a mess to clean up, and I don't have much time." He glared at Tracie. "So what's it going to be?"

"How can you hand me over to Trevor if he's in jail?"

"I have the power to free him. Besides, that's not

your concern. You simply have to decide—death or Trevor?"

"Death," Tracie retorted, refusing to look at her captor. Instead, she eyed Heath with a troubled look. Was she concerned for him? Or simply wary?

Jonas glanced between Tracie and Heath. "Oh, I see how it is. You prefer Heath over Trevor? He lied to you, Tracie. Heath lied."

"I don't care," Tracie snarled without looking at her captor, her eyes locked on Heath's face. "He's still a better man than Trevor."

The amused sound of Jonas' laughter caught Heath off guard. "You think so?" Jonas chuckled with an exaggerated sigh. "Heath, care to tell her the whole story? Who was the mole at the Coast Guard station—the person you were working so hard to flush out? Have you figured it out yet, Heath?"

Like a dying man whose life flashed before him, Heath replayed all the conversations he'd held with Jonas while on the Bayfield case. *Tracie's taking me by Trevor's house. We're meeting Tim tomorrow at noon. They moved Sal's transfer again.*

But Jonas had been in cahoots with Trevor all along, which explained why the other agents had been so confused when Heath had called from the boat and told them where to pick up Trevor. Jonas had given them other orders, had kept his own men out of Trevor's way and fed Tracie straight into their hands.

Just as Heath had blindly fed him the information he'd needed throughout the investigation. He'd given Tracie one more reason to hate him. Rather than give Jonas the satisfaction of telling her, Heath lifted his head and looked Jonas full in the face. When he spoke, his voice was full of self-loathing. "Me. I was the mole."

THIRTEEN

Though she knew it probably gave Jonas no end of satisfaction to hear it, Tracie couldn't suppress her gasp of surprise and disappointment at Heath's confession. He hadn't just betrayed her. He'd betrayed them all—Tim Price, Captain Sal, Gunnar, and everyone on the Bayfield Coast Guard team.

"Oh, I know," said Jonas in a fake commiserating voice, "it's so upsetting, isn't it? So you see, Tracie, Heath isn't worth dying for. I've made you an offer you can't refuse." He waved the handcuff key in her face. "Why don't you let me unchain you? We'll get you warmed up, find something to eat and get you back to Trevor where you belong."

Tracie looked up at him through angry eyes. The man was cruel—repulsively so. She couldn't stand that he'd killed her father. Worse than that, she couldn't tolerate the idea that he would kill her as well. She doubted there was anything she or Heath could do to free themselves, but she wasn't about to let Jonas get away with murder. As she lifted her head in defiance, she felt something sharp brush against her arm where it hung cuffed to the pipe above her.

Her hairclip.

The one with the recording transmitter. If Martina's explanation was correct, everything she heard all evening was being recorded and sent to a computer file with the FBI. Granted, if Jonas knew about the file he could have it deleted, but Tracie doubted he realized Martina had chosen to outfit her with the transmitter clip. Trevor's choice of jewelry removal had not been a coincidence— Jonas had probably told him exactly which pieces to take. Neither of them knew about the hairclip, she was certain. Martina had only added it at the last minute, apparently on a whim.

Tracie kept her expression neutral. All she needed to do was keep Jonas talking. The more information she could get him to spill, the more the FBI would have to use against him when it came time to lock him up. "Why do you care about what Trevor wants?"

She watched as her captor's lips thinned to a rumbling white line. "That's a long story."

"I've got time."

"Do you?" Jonas forced a laugh, as though he

found her statement ironic, but still felt reluctant to tell the story. "Only the time I give you."

Tracy wouldn't be intimidated. If the man wanted her to hook up with Trevor, he'd play along. *If* he really cared what Trevor wanted. "I don't understand," she baited him. "Why would such a high-ranking FBI official as yourself care what some low-life criminal wants? What does he have over you? Information?" She watched Jonas as the vein above his eye began to twitch.

She took that as affirmation that she was on the right track. "And so what if Trevor has dirt on you? Kill him."

"I tried that!" Jonas snapped back. "I shot him twice, right outside this cave. You saw his body floating in the water. And if I'd have left him there another couple of minutes, he'd be dead."

"So why didn't you leave him?"

The twitching trickled down from his eyelid to his mouth. Tracie watched as the FBI official fought between telling her and remaining silent. She prodded him with words. "If you wanted Trevor dead, why didn't you leave him? You had what you wanted."

"No, I didn't," Jonas cracked. "Trevor's father has too much on me—information that would put me away forever. If I let his son die, he'd expose me."

"So kill Tom Price, too. Kill them both."

"It's not that simple. I don't know where—" Jonas stopped mid-sentence, scowled and straightened. "Your choice is simple—Trevor or death." As he laid out her options, Jonas waggled the key at her once again.

Tracie wasn't satisfied. She wanted justice. If this man was going to kill her, she at least hoped to get him to spill enough of his secrets to put him away for life. She ignored his question. "How is it possible that you work for the FBI when you supposedly died on the *Requiem* twenty years ago? The FBI doesn't hire dead men. How did you outsmart the Navy and the FBI?"

As she watched, a light came on behind Jonas' eyes. Sinister pride glinted there, the kind of pride that couldn't resist a chance to boast. Tracie watched as Jonas made the decision to tell her everything. His chest puffed up slightly, and he tapped the key against his chin. He smiled to himself as he began his story.

"My name really *is* Jonas Goodman. I began working for the FBI twenty-six years ago. I started out like a lot of guys, naive, eager to please, ready to catch the bad guys and see good triumph over evil." He made a face. "That is, until I got smart. Figured out it doesn't work that way. I watched too many good men die poor and lonely trying to work for a thankless cause, and I decided that wouldn't be me.

"About that time, I was assigned to the coldest, loneliest spot on the Canadian border to investigate a customs issue involving some diamonds. Now, as I'm sure you're well aware, the border between Canada and the U.S. is friendly, but only if the personal effects a person carries are also the friendly sort. The government doesn't look too kindly on large amounts of diamonds sneaking through undeclared.

"I thought it was a chump assignment, and I won't pretend I wasn't offended to get it. But when I saw what these guys had, churning out diamonds by the bucketload, when I realized what kind of profit margins they could be capable of, I saw my ticket out of poor and lonely. I made a deal with the guys, bought them out, so to speak, in exchange for covering up what they'd done and covering our tracks for what we'd go on to do." Jonas chuckled to himself and continued.

"Of course, you can see the trouble. I bought them some time, but then what? How to shuttle that many diamonds across the border? Sure, Customs doesn't always check your bags, but they'd only have to crack open one suitcase and our gig would be up. And we couldn't just move our operation south—the raw materials we needed were abundant in Canada. Everything else was in place. We just needed a way to breach the border."

He smiled to himself as he paced before her, so

caught up in his self-glorifying tale he didn't even appear to suspect that he might be digging his own grave. His gravelly voice rumbled on. "About this time, I read about these shark class subs and realized they were just the ticket. Just what I needed. I took an extended leave of absence from the FBI and joined the Navy as Jonas Vaughn. Got myself assigned to this sub. Talked to the boys assigned with me. Tom and Mark, they were smart fellows, my right-hand men. Jeff Kuhlman, he never did take very well to the idea, needed too much encouragement, tended to get nervous about some of the things we'd done. And I can only put up with nervous folks for just so long.

"But the rest of us, we had a good run. I went back to being Jonas Goodman, went back to the FBI, took up right where I'd left off defending our nation from criminal activity, and always on the lookout for suspicious gems. As soon as some gemologist got too smart for his own good, tried to blow our cover, I had him blown first. It was a clean and tight operation. For over twenty years we kept it that way, and our blue diamonds have made us wealthy."

Jonas Goodman paused and looked back and forth between Heath and Tracie. "But some people don't kill too easy. They ask too many questions about things that aren't their business. And I tell you, kids, when I have to leave my office and come down here to clean things up myself, it makes me irritable. And when I get irritable, people don't die clean and easy. They die slow and ugly." He seemed to tire of his story then.

"So choose already! Are you going to go to Trevor, or am I going to have to kill you?"

"If you kill me, won't Trevor give away all your secrets?" Tracie asked. "He's been captured—won't he want to bargain for his freedom?"

For a second, Jonas looked like a trapped animal, but then pride filled his features again and his voice dropped to an even more threatening tone. "Fine. I'll make your choice easier for you. You can go to Trevor, or you can watch me kill Heath. I'll let you think about your decision a while."

He snapped off the light and slammed the door as he left, leaving them in utter darkness, which Tracie figured was just one small piece of his plan to leave them hopeless and helpless, just as she felt certain he wouldn't have risked telling them his tale unless he was absolutely certain they'd soon be dead.

Tracie felt her heart plunge to her knees. She might have been willing to die rather than become part of Trevor's criminal activities, but she couldn't imagine watching Jonas kill Heath. She'd crack. She couldn't see any way around it. They were both doomed.

"Tracie," Heath's whisper broke the silence. "Can you get your shoes off?"

His question seemed odd, but she answered, "I think so." A moment's foot-shuffling later, she announced. "Yes. They're off."

"Okay," Heath grunted. "I've shifted my body as close to you as I can. Reach out with your leg. I have Trevor's keys in my left pants pocket."

The darkness was complete, without the slightest hint of light. Tracie inched one foot toward Heath until she could feel the tips of his shoes with her toes. She strained the tight hold of her wrists against the pipes as she slid her foot up his leg until she found the opening to his pocket. It took several more minutes of shuffling, failed attempts before she caught the ring of keys with her toes and pulled them out.

Panting, she announced, "I've got them."

"Can you find the one you used earlier?"

"I'll try." Tracie recognized what Heath was getting at. He must have put Trevor's keys in his pocket before they'd left the speedboat. And since Jonas and his men had been playing friendly as they'd welcomed them aboard, they'd never patted them down, and the keys had gone unnoticed.

Which left them with a slim chance that the key she'd used to open her handcuffs at Trevor's would work on the cuffs Jonas had used on them—assuming Trevor and Jonas had used the same brand of cuffs, and assuming that brand was one that made all its cuffs with interchangeable locks. Though many of the major brands of handcuffs used interchangeable keys, some cuffs were made with unique keys, and if Trevor or Jonas had used that kind, there would be no way the key would open their cuffs—if they could even wrangle the key into the lock before Jonas or his men returned for them.

"I think I've got it," she announced, the slender key sliding between her first two toes as she flexed her foot against the cramp that had formed in her instep in protest of the unfamiliar activity.

"Can you hand it up to me?"

"I'll try." Grabbing hold with both hands to the bar she was cuffed to, Tracie pulled up her legs up like a monkey's while still clutching tight to the keys with her toes. She slid her feet along the pipe toward him, holding on to the heavy key ring with all the strength her foot could muster. As the cramp in her instep began to cry out, she felt her toes brush against metal.

And she dropped the keys.

They hit the floor with a loud clang, and Tracie froze, bracing herself as she waited for Jonas or one of his men to pounce.

"Here," Heath whispered. "I'm sliding them toward you on the floor. Try again—you were almost there."

Diligently, Tracie retrieved the keys and attempted the difficult maneuver a second time. This time, she felt his fingertips brush her toes as he took the keys from her with one hand. She dropped her feet to the floor and listened while Heath used the keys held in one hand to free his other wrist. A clicking sound told her when Heath's hand popped free.

"Praise God!" he declared, and a moment later she heard a second click. Instantly his warm hands found her in the cold darkness, feeling their way up her arms to the handcuffs that held her. Two clicks later, she sagged against Heath, taking just a moment to let the blood return to her arms. Then she found his ear in the darkness and whispered quietly, "Now what?"

Heath's lips grazed her earlobes and he held her tight against him as he spoke. "It won't be long before Jonas comes back. I say we wait and pounce. He's expecting us to be cuffed to the pipes. If we can catch him off guard—"

"But Jonas and his men are armed, and they also outnumber us," she said. What she really meant to say was that she didn't want to do any of it, but then she realized she had no choice. She shook her head. "The only way for this cup to pass is by our drinking it," she murmured.

"That sounds like something from the Bible," Heath murmured back.

"It is."

"Then that's what we're going to do," he announced decidedly. "I'm going to see if I can't brace myself close to the ceiling. Then I can drop on them when they walk in."

Tracie let out an exhausted sigh. "You can't be serious. Heath, you don't know how long it's going to be before Jonas and his men return. You could be holding on for hours." She shuddered at the thought, especially given his injuries. "Can't we just hide in the bunks and pull the curtains shut?"

"But won't that be the first place they look?"

"Sure, but we'll see them coming. That gives us an advantage."

"A small one," Heath conceded. "Okay, but I'll take the top bunk, you take the bottom one. Hopefully they'll check the middle one first. And let's just pray they don't come in shooting."

The bunks were stacked three high—Tracie figured a crew of four wouldn't need four bunks in the tightly-packed sub, since they'd rotate shifts for sleeping along with everything else. As she slid onto the soft blanket she whispered to Heath, "Let's pray we don't fall asleep, either. I'm so exhausted; it's going to be difficult to keep my eyes open. But if they walk in on us while we're asleep we'll lose everything we've gained."

"I'll keep you awake," he offered. "We need to

discuss our strategy. I'm going to strike first. You wait for my signal."

For several minutes, the two kept themselves awake by discussing what they'd do if Jonas came alone or with his men, how they'd disarm them, and under what circumstances they'd shoot. They both agreed not to kill the men unless they had no choice, preferring to see them face justice in court. Most importantly, they considered what to do once their captors were subdued—assuming they would be able to subdue them.

On a hunch, Heath rummaged in the darkness through the six-inch-deep drawers underneath the bunks. He gave a delighted cry when he discovered not only a flashlight, but extra handcuffs as well.

"Wonderful, now get back in your bunk and hide," Tracie hissed at him, though she felt encouraged by his find. God was providing for them.

Just as her exhaustion was beginning to overtake the adrenaline rush she'd felt since being captured, Tracie heard the taunting sound of Jonas Goodman's laughter echoing from the other side of the door. She braced herself and prayed.

As they'd planned, Heath waited for first Jonas and then the man behind him to step into the room. Jonas flicked on the light as he came in, which would have temporarily blinded them were it not for the filtering effect of the curtains that all but covered their bunks.

Tracie squinted at the light but heard a solid thump before the second man slumped to the floor. Jonas gave a cry, but it was cut short by a cracking sound Tracie hoped was Heath's shoe making contact with the killer's head. She didn't wait to find out, but swiftly swept her legs out, knocking the startled Jonas off his feet.

Tracie watched from a gap in the curtain of her bunk as Heath leapt down on top of Jonas, punched twice and then whispered to her, "They're both out. Cuffs?"

Springing from the bunk, Tracie worked quickly to cuff the men, and then searched their pockets thoroughly to be sure they didn't leave any keys on them. Then she and Heath said a quick prayer of thanks before proceeding down the passage toward the control room.

"Back so soon?" A swarthy Goliath chuckled at the sound of the door.

Instead of responding, Heath leapt toward the two men who sat obliviously with their backs to them. He'd removed his left shoe and hit them each in turn with the heel to their temples. When they slumped forward, he dragged them from their seats down the passage to the crew's quarters, where Jonas and the other man were still out cold. They cuffed them, patted down their pockets and locked the door behind them.

"Now," Heath said, racing back to the control

room, "let's sort out where we are and figure out if we can drive this thing. I want to get back to Bayfield before those guys have time to give us any more trouble."

Heath looked over the controls with a sinking heart. As he'd feared, the multimillionaire smugglers hadn't been content to leave the government-issued sub controls alone. They'd had a custom job installed, with more bells and whistles and newer technology than anything he'd ever seen. He had a sudden flashback of the trouble he'd experienced adapting to the unfamiliar control panel on the microwave at his Bayfield apartment. And the submarine controls were a thousand times more complicated.

"Can I help?" Tracie asked, hovering at his elbow.

Desperately, Heath tried to recognize something familiar among the instruments before him. "You can pray."

Her small hand slid over his fingers. "You pray with me, okay?"

With their foreheads just touching, they thanked God for getting them as far as he had. Heath tried not to let on to Tracie just how desperate their situation was. They were lost in the dark, silent lake, and he had no idea how far they'd gone from the Devil's Island sea cave, or in what direction, let alone how fast they were going or whether they were even moving at all. The waters that had once claimed her father's life could very well still claim theirs.

"Amen," they said together, and Heath prepared to admit to Tracie that he didn't know what he was doing.

Before he could speak, she leaned toward the large grid-filled screen that dominated the controls, her eyes smiling. "This is so amazing," she whispered.

"Yeah," he agreed, unsure what had captured her awe. "What is?"

"Their depth-chart map. It's so detailed, so complete. They've got the whole lake here. And look." She touched the screen and swept her hands gently up, and watched the picture move up with her movement. When she slid her hand sideways, the picture moved from side to side. She tapped a spot on the screen, and the image zoomed forward. Her voice carried an air of discovery. "You can zoom in on any part of the map." She slid the picture sideways and tapped the screen a few times, snapping the focus tighter with every tap of her fingertip. "There's Devil's Island."

"So you know where we are?" Heath asked, hardly daring to hope that Tracie had recognized what he had been unable to see.

"Well, if that's us," she said zooming out again

and touching the screen below a blinking red dot. Suddenly the screen changed to a picture of a shark class submarine. "And I think it is," she continued, tapping the screen again and sending them back to a panoramic view, "then we're right here."

Heath looked at the fresh picture on the screen in wonder. "And where is here?"

"The bottom of the North Channel, just off Madeline Island. About a mile from Bayfield."

The news was better than Heath had dared to hope. He had a fighting chance of navigating them into pier. "Any idea how deep we are?"

Tracie clicked through the screens. "I don't know." She paused on the depth chart. "It almost seems as though we're on the surface," she said, zooming in on their sub, then panning back out as far as the screens would take her.

"Perfect!" Heath wanted to kiss her, but the way she'd been cold to him all evening, he doubted it would endear him to her. Probably the opposite. Instead he crossed the room to where the periscope hung from the ceiling. At least the smugglers hadn't messed with the manual controls. "I should be able to bring her in from here."

Just as Heath was about to situate himself at the controls, he heard a distant thunk.

He looked into Tracie's concerned face. "What do you suppose that was?"

"Our friends must be waking up," Tracie speculated.

"You stay right here," Heath insisted. "I'm going to go check on them."

He hurried down the hall, peeking into the darkened crew's quarters just long enough to be sure his eyes hadn't deceived him. Then he ran back to the control room, taking care to lock the door securely behind him.

"What did you find?" Tracie asked.

"Those three big guys are still out cold," Heath assured her.

"Is Jonas awake?"

"He must be. He wasn't in the room."

Tracie felt her heart tap-dancing with fear against her ribs. "Where could he be?"

"Anywhere. He could be sneaking up on us this very minute. If we're at the surface, he could escape through another hatch, pop out a life raft and disappear. Anything is possible."

"We can't let him get away." Tracie looked over the myriad instruments that covered the walls and even the ceiling of the small room. "You think you can drive this thing?"

"Oh, yeah."

"Get us into port as fast as you can. I'm going to try to contact somebody on shore. They need to be on the lookout for Jonas."

While Heath did his thing at the periscope, Tracie frantically started trying instruments. She found a microphone behind a hidden panel, but when she spoke into it, she only heard her own voice blaring back at her. "Intercom," she concluded, slamming it shut again.

Finally she tried a smaller screen, which proved to be equipped with the same touch screen capabilities as the larger one on the wall. "Yes!" she announced after a couple of clicks, "we've got Internet access. Must be a satellite connection."

"What are you going to do?" Heath asked. "E-mail the Coast Guard for help?"

"Too slow," she clucked at him as she typed in their call for help. "Instant messaging." A moment later, their SOS was sent, and she closed her eyes, praying it would reach help in time.

"Tracie," Heath's fingers brushed her hand and she nearly jumped.

"What?"

"I've got us parked in the docking bay next to the Coast Guard building. I'm going to open the hatch."

"And?" She wondered what the intense look he gave her was all about.

"There's some possibility, if Jonas hopped out another hatch, that he could be lying in wait for us the second we open this one."

FOURTEEN

Tracie swallowed hard, immediately recognizing the danger they were in. She linked her fingers around Heath's. "Let's pray."

They bent their heads together, and while Heath begged for God's protection, Tracie felt her heart melting toward him. She knew she'd fallen in love with her Coast Guard partner, and had to remind herself that the man in front of her was essentially a stranger. She'd fallen in love with his act, not a real man.

When he whispered "Amen," and looked at her with smoldering eyes, Tracie had to force herself to turn away and look up the ladder to the main hatch, telling herself there was nothing real behind his facade. She took a step toward the ladder. "Okay. Let's go."

Heath didn't let go of her fingers, but instead gently tugged her back.

"What?" she asked.

"Me first," he insisted.

"Fine." She looked at him patiently, waiting, far more aware of him than she wanted to be. The fine smile lines around his eyes were too familiar to her, the hint of a dimple on his cheek, the curvature of his jaw line were all indelibly imprinted in her heart. And yet, she knew the man before her was actually a stranger. She didn't even know where his cover story ended and the real Heath began. She doubted she'd ever get to meet the real Heath.

It hadn't escaped her attention that once they stepped out of the submarine, they'd have no reason to ever see each other again. Heath would no doubt go back to his real job at the FBI. She'd stay in the Coast Guard. The thought made her feel cold.

For a long time, he made no move, but only gazed back at her. Finally he let out a sigh. "Are you going to hate me forever?"

"I'm tired. My feet hurt, I'm cold, I just want out of here. I want done with this."

He reached for her, smoothing back an errant strand of hair and tucking it behind her ear. "I owe you an explanation."

His expression was too intense. She closed her eyes against it. "Not right now. Let's just get out of here before something else goes wrong."

"I don't want to leave things like this between us."

His voice was gentle, almost pleading, and far too similar to what she'd heard when he'd first wriggled his way past her defenses and into her heart. She steeled her resolve against him. Popping her eyes open, she glared at him. "There's nothing you can say that's going to fix it. So either you climb up that ladder, or I'll go first."

Heath didn't protest any longer, but showed her how to release the hatch once he was poised to look out. If the coast was clear, he'd climb out and she'd be free to ascend after him. If anything looked amiss, he'd pull the lid down—hopefully before Jonas could get off a shot.

Tracie waited patiently while he poked his head up.

"See anything?" she asked as his feet moved another step upward.

"Come on up," he called down to her.

Tracie clambered up the rungs and poked her head out. The rosy glow of dawn cut through the eastern foggy haze, and the first thing she saw was the welcome sight of land, the Coast Guard building, and her fellow crewmen standing on the dock, their faces slack-jawed.

Then Tracie turned around and saw what they were gaping at.

The six hydraulic missile doors on the rear end

of the sub stood open. Instead of armaments, the compartments were each heaped with sparkling diamonds.

"Oh," Tracie could hardly fathom how many gems there must be inside the compartments. Thousands upon thousands—millions, even.

"Tell me those aren't real," Jim called from the dockside.

"Depends on what you consider real, my friend," Heath called back. At the sound of his voice, Tracie turned to him and realized he was waiting with his arm outstretched, ready to help her up. She tentatively took his hand and stepped into the sunlight.

"Any word on Jonas?"

Heath shook his head. "I need to get some men down there and look for him."

Tracie instinctively placed her hand on his arm as if to restrain him, but caught herself before she asked him not to go. She told herself she didn't need to be concerned for his safety. He was only doing his job. Besides, she couldn't allow herself to care for him any more.

Tracie hurried down off the sub. "Jake," she called, turning to the Officer in Charge. "We've captured four men on board. Three of them are handcuffed in the crew's quarters. The fourth is at large on the ship, unless he snuck out through an escape hatch before we discovered he was missing."

"I'm on it," Jake replied with a nod. "What's he look like?"

"You've met him once before. Jonas Goldman, a.k.a. Jonas Vaughn—" she paused, watching Jake's face "—a.k.a. Jonas Blaine."

Recognition dawned on her superior officer's features. "He was on the sub." Jake turned and looked at the *Requiem*. "He was on *that* sub, the day…" His voice faded.

Tracie nodded solemnly. "Jonas killed my father. Don't let him get away."

Jake nodded and quickly began issuing instructions to his men, who met Heath just as he was disembarking the sub. Tracie realized she must look ridiculous in her rumpled dress, with Heath's tuxedo jacket hanging off her shoulders. Worse than that, she felt exhausted. But at the same time, she wasn't about to leave until she was sure Jonas had been caught.

She watched as Heath led a group of men back down the hatch. After several agonizing minutes, four Coast Guardsmen emerged with three thugs cuffed between them.

Jonas didn't come out. Neither did Jake or Heath.

Tracie fidgeted, pulling the blanket tight against the winter cold, her eyes trained on the sub, scanning it for any sign of movement, any indication that would tell her what was going on inside. The sea monster sat silent, unmoving.

Where was Heath? What was happening to him? She told herself she didn't care, that it didn't matter to her what happened to him, that the man inside the submarine was a stranger to her, and her concern for him was no more than she would feel for any other human being. He was no one special.

Then she heard a muffled shout from inside, and a moment later Jim's head popped up the hatch. "Medics! We need medical assistance!"

Tracie rushed forward, but her fellow crewmen had already stowed the other thugs inside their vehicles, and they rushed past her and poured down the hatch. A short while later they led Jonas out. She watched as they escorted her father's killer away.

"Lord, please, *please*," she begged under her breath, her prayer more heartfelt cry than conscious thought. She hesitated on the edge of the dock, itching to climb back down in the sub and find out what was going on, but at the same time, certain she'd only be in the way.

Wailing sirens announced the arrival of the paramedic team. Tracie stepped to the side as the medics in their bright orange jumpsuits hurried over. For a few long minutes, they clambered up and down. Then, finally, a man popped out and reached down as another lifted up the end of a stretcher.

Jake.

His face was ashen, but he appeared to be conscious. The crowd of men around him made it difficult for Tracie to assess his injuries. Though she felt concern for the man who'd once been her father's best friend, it looked as though he'd be okay. But what had become of Heath?

After helping the men secure Jake to the stretcher, Heath stood back and waited for them to lift him up the hatch. It was tricky work, especially since they didn't want to jostle him. Finally the sub was empty, and he followed the last man up the ladder.

The dock swarmed with officers, medics, and curious bystanders who were being kept at bay by a strand of hastily installed crime scene tape. Still, it wasn't difficult for him to spot Tracie. She was the only person standing still, her eyes glued to the spot where he emerged. For one heart-warming moment, he thought he saw relief cross her features. Then she turned her back on him and hurried away.

Tracie slept more than thirty hours over the next two days. When she wasn't asleep, the guys from the Coast Guard kept her updated on all that had happened. Trevor and his father were awaiting trial alongside Mark Smith, a.k.a. Mark Anderson, as well as Jonas and the twenty other men they'd nabbed in relationship to the case. Martina, Oleg and Olaf were on leave pending an investigation of their relationship to Jonas. They'd already turned in the transmitted recording of Jonas's confession, which indicated they were likely innocent of any intentional conspiracy, but had simply been following orders.

Jake quickly bounced back from the bullet that had grazed his leg, though the Coasties speculated it might take him a little longer to get over all the fuss his men had made when they'd discovered he was wounded.

While she was recuperating at her parents' house, Tracie found an old home video of her father's birthday party the night before the sub had disappeared halfway around the world, and watched as Jake sang "Happy Birthday" to her father, along with Jim, and even Joe Cooper, who'd been a hunting pal of her dad's long before he'd married Malcolm's widow. So she didn't have to feel even the slightest residual suspicion toward the men in her life whose first initial was the letter J.

Gunnar came home with a pronounced limp and quickly claimed Heath's tuxedo jacket as his new favorite blanket. Tracie tried to tell herself she didn't care if he took it, but when he laid his head on the jacket, looked up at her with sad eyes and whimpered mournfully, she couldn't help but pat him on the head and whisper, "I miss him, too. But he was never really who we thought he was."

A week passed. Two weeks. Tracie went back to work, but now that her father's killer had been caught, she felt as though her mission had been accomplished. Still, she wasn't sure what she would do if she gave up working for the Coast Guard. All her training, all her life's ambitions from the time her father died had been focused on becoming a Coastie. She didn't know anything else.

Part of her wondered what Heath was up to, but she heard nothing from him or about him. Whatever emotions she'd felt toward him obviously couldn't have been love. She didn't even know the real Heath Gerlach, and he obviously wasn't coming back.

That didn't make it any easier for her to forget him.

The more she thought about him, the angrier she felt. He'd emotionally manipulated her and used her to learn whatever information he was after. She didn't know if anything they'd shared between them had been real. Even when she thought about the discussions they'd shared about faith, she felt foolish knowing she'd spoken from the heart, while all the while he'd been investigating her. When she'd started hoping they might have a future together, he'd only been trying to get the assignment over with.

After all she'd been through, it wasn't Trevor's cruelty or the *Requiem*'s long subversive presence that left her crying on her pillow at night. Her greatest pain came from thinking about Heath. She couldn't seem to get over her love for him.

Her greatest solace was teaching the self-defense class at the rec center. Tracie asked the staff about adding more courses. The manager agreed that her class was popular, but since the Northwoods experienced a significant population drop every winter, she suggested waiting until summer before adding another class.

Which left Tracie standing alone after class the next Tuesday night, practicing her moves on a padded dummy. As she completed a complex series of kicks, she heard a coughing sound behind her. At first she just assumed it was one of the ladies from her class stopping by to say good-night after a swim or a cool-down on the treadmill.

But when she turned around, she saw the man she'd just envisioned herself attacking.

"Heath?"

"Hey—"

She cut him off immediately. "What are you doing here?"

"I thought I'd—"

She cut him off again. "I don't want to talk to you. I don't want to see you."

He advanced toward her slowly. "But I was hoping—"

"Don't," she insisted, her eyes firmly on him. It was one thing to work out her anger on the dummy. It was another thing entirely to face the man, smile crinkles, dimple and all.

He continued moving toward her. "Tracie, I really need—"

She couldn't let him continue. "I'm warning you, Heath, now is really not a good time."

"Then when is a good time?" He paused.

"Never." She stared him down, wishing the skipping in her heart was entirely from anger, and not just the unnerving way her heart had always leapt at the sight of him.

"Then it seems now is just as good a time as any." He took another step toward her.

Setting her face in a scowl, she came at him as though to kick him. When he covered his ribs to block her, she dropped her fake, and released her back fist on his jaw.

His eyes brightened. "I suppose I deserved that."

She faked again, this time as though to deliver another back fist, but the moment he drew his hands up, she kicked him in the ribs.

Surprise and a hint of a smile showed on his

face, and he raised his arms in a blocking stance. "You want to play?" he asked.

"I'm not playing," she shot back, punctuating each word with a reverse punch in his gut.

"You're mad at me," he stated flatly, unaffected by what she considered to be some pretty powerful blows—and he wasn't even wearing body armor. His impassivity only irritated her more. She threw a round kick toward his head.

He blocked it. "You have every reason to be mad at me." He blocked the next two kicks she sent toward him, then dropped his arms. "You know what? Fine. Get it out of your system."

Tracie narrowed her eyes. "What?"

"Kick me. Hit me. Whatever. I don't blame you for being angry at me. *I'm* angry at me for what I did."

For a moment, she relaxed her guard, but when he moved to step closer to her, she planted a few more punches in his midsection. "Why did you come back?" she asked, pummeling him.

"Because I love you."

Her foot flew fast toward his head, but he caught it in his hand.

She tried to wiggle her sneaker from his grip, and nearly lost her balance as she stood on one foot, glaring at him. "No, you don't."

"I do," he said simply, and let go of her shoe.

"No, you don't!" she insisted, coming at him

with both fists, thumping his ribs until she sagged against him, weak and out of breath.

He supported her arms and looked her full in the face. "I love you."

"No, you don't." She twisted free and swept one leg behind him, knocking him down on one knee.

He looked up at her but didn't move to stand. "Have you finally got me where you want me?"

With a disgusted grumble, Tracie turned and stomped away.

Heath stood and trotted after her. "I brought you something."

She ignored him and kept walking toward the front doors.

"It's out here." Heath tugged at her arm.

She followed quietly at a distance, hardly believing he'd really come back, completely unsure how to respond to his claims of love after all the emotional upheaval she'd been through.

He stepped outside, where the gentle snow fell in swirling crystalline array, coating the street and the sidewalk like so many diamonds. He strode to his truck. She was surprised to see it was the same vehicle he'd driven while undercover. Perhaps not everything she'd known about him had been false. He pulled a large silver case from the passenger side and popped it open.

"Behold, the newest line of tools in the Gerlach family—the diamond series."

She looked down and blinked at the sparkling tools, each studded with diamonds above the grips on the handles.

He extended the open case toward her. "It's for you."

Though she wished she could pretend to be ambivalent toward him, her curiosity got the better of her. She reached out a tentative hand. "Are these," she ran one finger along a line of gems, "are these what I think they are?"

"They're synthetic diamonds of the highest quality, chemically, optically and in all other ways identical to the real thing, except that these little buggers were grown in a lab."

"Where did you get them?"

"Government auction." He grinned at her. "It seems the FBI confiscated two tons of these little guys. They didn't need them all as evidence, and you'd be surprised what a deal I got on them since they aren't really real. Of course, I had to sign a letter of intent stating that I wouldn't try to pass them off as the real thing. No one seemed to know what to do with them since they couldn't be sold as natural diamonds, but I'd been thinking about how I was going to start my new job at Gerlach Tools, and it seemed launching a new product line would be a fitting way to begin."

She pulled her hand away slowly, her memories of Trevor's gala catching up to her. "So they're blue diamonds?"

"No," Heath assured her, popping out a light, which he flicked on. "These are from the new violet line that Trevor never got around to announcing."

As he waved the black light across their surface, the diamonds phosphoresced with a faint purple glow. Tracie smiled slowly.

"Do you like them?" Heath asked in a soft voice.

Unsure what to say, Tracie looked into his face. "Is this what you've been up to for the last two weeks?"

"That and fighting pneumonia."

"You had pneumonia?" Immediately Tracie felt guilty. She hadn't even known. "Why didn't you tell me?"

"Why? What would you have done?"

Her mouth fell open and she tried to process an answer, but none seemed to fit. She wouldn't have gone to visit him, would she? "How bad was it?" she asked.

Heath laughed, but his laughter quickly morphed into a fit of coughing. "After everything I'd been through—" he coughed again, his blue eyes melting into hers "—pretty bad."

"I thought you were invincible." She couldn't keep the concern from her voice.

"Turns out I'm not after all."

Her heart wrenched at his admission, and she gave up trying to stifle her curiosity about what had happened to him. "So, you're not at the FBI anymore?"

"No." Heath looked at her levelly. "I thought I'd lose my job after bucking the order to come in, but since Jonas Goodman is behind bars now, none of his orders stand. Turns out the Bureau was pretty glad I stepped in and picked up the slack. They offered me my boss's job."

"I'm confused," Tracie admitted, not sure what he was trying to tell her.

"I didn't take it." Heath looked down at the diamond-studded tools he held, and his voice sounded hoarse as he explained, "I had a lot of fun working for the FBI, but I realized I'd been running from my family for too long. I resented not really knowing my parents growing up, but by refusing to forgive them, I denied myself the opportunity to get to know them." Heath shifted the tools to one hand and reached for her, "I want to settle down, to raise a family, to carry on the family business for another generation."

Tracie's throat swelled, and she didn't trust herself to speak. Maybe the Heath she'd fallen in love with hadn't been a cover after all. Maybe she'd fallen in love with the real man.

Heath started to close the tool case, but then paused, looked at her, looked down at the tools, and then opened the case again. "Not all of these are violet diamonds." He reached toward a large gem that sat in the center of the display. "This one here wasn't grown in a lab. God made it." He held up a diamond solitaire ring. "And I'd like you to have it, but only—" He paused, his voice so husky she could barely make out his words. He set the rest of the tool kit behind him.

Lowering himself down on one knee, he took her hand. "Only if you'll marry me."

Tracie looked at him, and all the anger and disappointment she'd felt at his betrayal suddenly felt like far too heavy a burden to bear. She didn't want to stay mad at him. The last thing she wanted to do was to deny herself the opportunity to love him by refusing to forgive him. No, she wanted to love him forever and always. It was all she could do to nod and reach for the ring.

Heath stood and slid it onto her finger, then kissed her.

She kissed him back, and finally felt as though all the uncertainties of the future before her had found their answer. When he pulled back, she looked at the brilliant ring. "It fits perfectly. How did you know my size?"

"Jake ratted you out."

Tracie had heard that line before. She laughed and kissed him again, unmindful of the thick snow that had begun to fall and stick to them.

"Oh, sure, they're just partners, she says." The purple-suited figure stopped behind them, blew out an exasperated breath, and walked on to her car. "Young people these days!"

"He's not my partner anymore," Tracie called after her. "He's my fiancé!" Then she threw back her head and laughed with Heath until he pulled her into his arms and kissed her again.

* * * * *

Dear Reader,

I've had so much fun revisiting my Devil's Island characters and helping Tracie Crandall find her happily ever after with Heath. Tracie has learned to be a tough, no-nonsense kind of girl, but once Heath breaks through her defenses, he finds a frightened woman in need of a friend. Heath has put up his own walls—blocking his family, and keeping out God. As they learn to trust one another, their love blossoms.

Tracie and Heath were very enjoyable characters for me to work with, because I was able to emphasize strongly with each of them. In fact, I think many of us have put up emotional barriers in our lives from time to time, pushing people away so we can't be hurt again. These walls aren't necessarily a bad thing—sometimes we just need time to heal. But if we cower for too long behind our defenses, we can miss out on the good gifts God is trying to give us, just as Heath and Tracie almost missed out on the their love for each other.

I hope you've enjoyed reading about Heath and Tracie! I have more romantic adventures in the works. Check out my Web site at www.rachellemccalla.com for news about upcoming new releases, as well as fun background articles on the people and places in my books! And feel free to drop a comment in my blog—I love hearing from readers!

Rachelle

QUESTIONS FOR DISCUSSSION

1. Because of his investigation, Heath wasn't allowed to tell Tracie who he really worked for. How do you feel about his deception? Do you believe he made the right choice? Why or why not?

2. Tracie is initially very cold toward Heath because of her previous experiences with Trevor. Do you believe her behavior is justifiable? Does it make you respect her more or less?

3. Does anyone in your life make an exaggerated effort to keep you at arm's length as Tracie did with Heath? Do you treat anyone this way? What are the benefits and costs of this kind of behavior?

4. At the start of the story, Tracie has few friends or family members she is close to. How does this make her more vulnerable? What would you have done differently in her shoes?

5. When Heath shows up at her house with pizza, Tracie lets him in, in spite of her personal policy against fraternizing with her coworkers.

Do you think she made the right choice? Why or why not?

6. As Heath begins to care for Tracie, he realizes he's lost his ability to objectively evaluate her as a suspect—in other words, his feelings for her make him more likely to overlook indications that she might be guilty. Have you ever experienced something similar? Do you tend to favor the people you are close to over others? In what ways is that a good thing? In what ways might it be bad?

7. As Heath and Tracie make their dive, Heath observes that Tracie's smaller, more nimble shape is better suited to diving, whereas his strength is an advantage on land. What other differing gifts did you observe between them? How does this strengthen them as a team? What challenges does it present?

8. Heath insisted on working even though he was wounded. Do you think he made the right choice? Why or why not?

9. Tracie begins to trust Heath in part because her dog, Gunnar, likes him. Do you think this is a solid basis for her trust? How would you have behaved in the same situation?

10. When Heath risks his life to rescue Gunnar, Tracie realizes she shouldn't have asked him to endanger himself for her dog. Do you agree or disagree, and why?

11. Heath resents the fact that his parents weren't available to him as a child. Have you ever had similar feelings toward a significant person in your life? How does Heath overcome his resentment? Do you agree with Heath's decision to go back home and run the family business?

12. Tracie says that God can take things other people meant for evil, and turn the into something good (see *Romans* 8:28). Do you believe this is true? In what ways has God taken negative experiences in your life and made them turn out for good?

13. Heath imagines that God is too busy for him because his parents were too busy for him growing up. In what ways has your relationship or lack of relationship with your parents influenced your attitude toward God? In what ways has this been good? In what ways bad?

14. Tracie's faith is the foundation of her life. Because of this, she has determined she can't

be in an intimate relationship with a man who doesn't have a relationship with God—which means she initially can't date Heath. Do you agree with her decision? What are the benefits and costs of her decision? What would you do differently?

15. Tracie has learned self-defense to protect herself, and uses her moves at various points throughout the book. Do you feel this is appropriate for a Christian woman in her position? How might you have behaved differently?

HEARTWARMING INSPIRATIONAL ROMANCE

Contemporary,
inspirational romances
with Christian characters
facing the challenges
of life and love
in today's world.

NOW AVAILABLE IN REGULAR AND LARGER-PRINT FORMATS.

Steeple
Hill®

Love Inspired.
HISTORICAL
INSPIRATIONAL HISTORICAL ROMANCE

Engaging stories of romance,
adventure and faith,
these novels are set in
various historical periods
from biblical times
to World War II.

NOW AVAILABLE!

Steeple
Hill®